Redeer

MW01493641

Cyborg Seduction - Book Six

By Laurann Dohner

Redeeming Zorus

by Laurann Dohner

Charlie's brother has put her in the no-win situation of having to rescue a cyborg from Earth Government. It's dangerous, she'll become an outlaw on Earth, but it's the only way to save her brother's life. The imprisoned cyborg is rude, conceited and probably the biggest jerk she's ever had the misfortune to meet. His *only* redeeming qualities are his handsome face and sexy, muscular body. Just wow! Still, she can't wait to be rid of him.

All cyborgs hate humans, but Zorus is consumed by it. Chained, enslaved and facing death on Earth once again, he vows revenge. To his utter astonishment, a human female comes to his rescue. She's rude, mouthy and bossy. And very brave. She baffles him almost as much as she arouses him. Zorus cannot deny that he's fascinated by her. They are about to lock wills and ignite a firestorm of desire that defies every rule he lives by.

Dedication:

To Mr. Laurann, for all the wonderful ways he supports me.

Cyborg Seduction Series

Redeeming Zorus

Editor: Kelli Collins

Cover Art: Dar Albert

eBook ISBN: 978-1-944526-73-3

Prologue

"You've got to be kidding me." Charlie glared at her brother. "No way in hell."

"They are willing to pay a fortune if we do this. We'd be set for life, could leave Earth, and go settle on Saturn. It's not a shithole and did I mention how much money these guys offered to rescue this thing?"

"We couldn't spend a credit of it even if I could pull it off because dead people don't buy stuff, Russell. We'd be fugitives and if you think I could get that thing out of there without tipping them off that I'm the one who did it, think again. I know the security measures they have since I installed most of them."

"That's why you're the only person who can do it, Charlie. Come on, baby sis." He gave her a pleading look.

"Stop it. That doesn't work on me."

An annoyed look twisted his features. "I gave my word we'd do it."

"We? You mean me. You were wrong." She ran her fingers through her thick, dark hair to push it over her shoulder and then shook her head. "I worked really hard to get where I am." She glanced around their small apartment. "It's not much but we're not scraping by inside hovels anymore. We're living in a good part of the city where we're safe from thieves. Nobody can get past those guards outside."

Russell bit his lip. "I already took the money. I told them there would be upfront costs involved. If I don't deliver the cyborg, they'll kill me. I know

7

you're going to tell me to return the deposit but it's been spent. I lost it gambling."

She had to take deep breaths to control the anger boiling up. She counted to ten silently. "Damn you," she hissed. "I worked my butt off to get us out of the trouble you kept finding when we were kids. I should allow them kill you."

"I'm all you've got and you love me." He gave her a knowing smirk. "There'll be enough money involved that Earth Government can't touch us on Saturn."

"You're an idiot. Of course they can. They'll just hire assassins to come after us. That's what they do when you screw with them. They are really excited about this cyborg they captured. He doesn't appear to have aged since he escaped Earth a long time ago. Do you get that? They aren't going to shrug this off. He's pure gold to those scientists. It's the most animated I've ever seen those jerks since I started to work there."

"I know I'm not as smart as you." Bitterness tinged his voice. "But I gave my word to break him out when I took their money. You have to do this or you're killing me."

She closed her eyes, fighting tears. It had fallen onto her to take care of her older brother after their parents had been killed when she was fifteen. Russell had issues with gambling, he always ran his mouth, and it had been one bad situation after another.

The cyborg was a huge discovery since they were supposed to be extinct, thanks to Earth Government having killed them all decades before. Whoever had paid her brother probably valued it as much as the scientists at the Earth Government-run Gorman Medical Facility. The cyborg might be some kind of miracle cure for aging if the doctors could just figure it out.

"Charlie? I love you. I know you'll do the correct thing."

Her eyes snapped open to glare at him. "If that were true, I wouldn't have brought you with me when I landed the job at the facility and earned the transfer to the safer side of the city. Of course those guys you owed money would have killed you if I hadn't. Now you're causing me more problems. When is it enough with you? Don't you ever get tired of ruining my life? I work hard to give us a better one but you seem just as determined to screw it up."

"They'll kill me and those guards downstairs won't be able to stop them. You and I both know they'll just bribe them to get at me, with the kind of money they have."

"Fuck!" She sat hard in a chair and shot him another glare. "I want you to know, if we survive this, if we manage to get off Earth alive, I'm done. Do you hear me? We'll split the money and then you're on your own. I love you but I'm not allowing you to take me down with you again. You've obviously got a death wish but I want to keep breathing."

"It hurts me to hear you say that."

"It hurts me every time you get us into one of these messes."

"You can do anything you set your mind to." He inched closer to give her the look she hated most. It was the one that reminded her of when they'd been kids and he'd still been the brother she loved so deeply. "I knew you'd do the right thing for me."

She stood. "Shut up. I have to plan on how to get that thing out of there." She paused. "He's dangerous. For all I know, he'll kill me the second I get him free. Did you think of that?"

"Tell him the council paid you for breaking him out and you're the one who is going to get him off Earth. They said he'd know you were friendly then."

"What council?" An uneasy feeling surfaced inside Charlie.

"I have no idea. That was the message they gave me to relay so he knows you're really there to help him."

"Who are these people?"

Russell shrugged. "I didn't ask."

"Maybe they are bullshitting you about the rest of the money. Did you ever think of that?"

"I'm not totally stupid. I had them put it into a trust."

"Shit." She shook her head. "And who is the controller of it? Some lowlife you used to run with who is going to steal it?"

"It's Gerald."

Pain sliced through Charlie at the mere mention of his name. "Oh."

"He won't steal from us. He still feels real bad about what he did to you."

Hot tears burned behind her eyes. "How is his rich wife?"

"He hates her."

"Good." She decided a little satisfaction had to be better than none at all. "He doesn't need to steal. He already gave up his soul for all the money he could ever spend."

"He loves you."

"Shut up. He made his choice when he dumped me for that rich bitch. Let's not say his name again. That's the rule, remember?"

"You asked."

"I did. My mistake." She ran her fingers through her hair again, a habit she hated but couldn't break, surprised she had any left after years of her brother making her tear at it. "Let me think. I need to come up with a plan."

"They want him out fast, Charlie. I told them you could do it within twenty-four hours."

"Are you high?" She yelled but then remembered the walls weren't that thick and they had nosy neighbors. Her voice lowered. "There's no way—"

"They have a ship waiting and ready to take him off Earth. We're supposed to rendezvous with it at seven tomorrow evening. They bribed officials to allow it to lift off without being searched first. They also booked us passage on another ship where they won't check our identities in case they immediately figure out who took him. This is all going to work out great. It's going to be easy money."

"Great. I'll just sprout wings while I'm doing the impossible, fly in and grab him, and we'll just sail out of there."

"Smart ass."

"Dumb ass."

Russell grinned. "I love you."

"You're lucky we're blood, Russell. That's all I have to say. Now shut up and let me think."

Chapter One

Crazy. Insane. Nuts. This will never work. I need my head examined. Those were the thoughts that ran through Charlie's head while she listened to Doctors Barklin and Aims argue.

"The only way we're going to figure this out is by autopsy."

"What if that doesn't work? We don't have a large supply of them anymore to run tests on. If more of them exist, that thing isn't talking. We'll have lost the only live opportunity to study him if you're wrong."

"The autopsy will work," Doctor Barklin grumbled. "I can do extensive studies on the cyborg's body. I believe the brain slice samples alone will unlock the mystery."

Nausea settled in Charlie's stomach at hearing them speak so callously about killing the cyborg. She'd never tolerated the scientists much and knew it was a mutual hatred. Their utter lack of compassion left her cold inside, wondering if they considered her subhuman as well. She was just a tech-head who ran their security upgrades and kept their machines up and running—a nobody in their world.

Both doctors had been raised in the better parts of town, had access to education levels she'd only dreamed about. She owed it to the kindness of rich people for the skills she had learned as a teen. Someone had taken pity on her, deemed her cute, and life had improved with their generosity when they had donated a scholarship for her schooling. Of course that had only gotten her so far with the "well off" population. Everyone at the facility knew she'd been raised in the slums.

"I say we wait and run more live tests." Doctor Aims whined when he spoke. "If I don't get significant results we could do it your way. I know you're impatient but the risks are just too great if you're wrong. We need to play this safe."

"Fine," Barklin snapped. He turned in his chair to glare at Charlie. "What do you want, grunt?"

She hated the title they'd dubbed her, a constant reminder of her low status. "It's time for the security upgrades." She glanced at her watch. "Of course you could complain to the director who scheduled them if you don't agree with the timing. I hear he hates to be disturbed during his dinner break but it's your ass he'll chew, not mine."

Aims paled slightly, obviously not thrilled with that prospect. "No one mentioned it to us. It's marked on the schedule for tomorrow evening."

"That's not my problem." She shrugged. "I'm just a grunt, remember?" She enjoyed the annoyed look they shared when she tossed their title back in their usually smug faces. "I just follow orders."

Both men stood. Doctor Aims leered at her when he passed, his gaze lowering to her breasts. "Really? So if I tell you to—"

"I wouldn't finish that sentence," she interrupted. "You know where I grew up and I'll remove any of your body parts you tell me to touch. It wouldn't be the first time some idiot bled over making that mistake."

"Bitch," he muttered, leaving the room quickly to follow Barklin.

14

Charlie dropped into one of their chairs and started typing at a terminal the moment they cleared the room. In seconds the screen in front of her showed the holding cell where the cyborg had been detained. She openly gawked at her first glimpse of him.

He appeared huge on the monitor, mostly naked except for a pair of baggy black shorts, and they had him chained against a wall. Muscles and dusky, smooth, silvery-gray skin were plentiful for her to gape at. His hair hung to his shoulders in a tangled mess. The lighting inside the cell had to be harsh on his eyes, would be on anyone's under the too-bright illumination.

Charlie bit her lip as she pulled up the tracking system that monitored all the employees on the basement floor of the building where she sat. Two signals moved toward the break room, she assumed it had to be the doctors, while three more life signs registered inside the security room two corridors over. One additional one showed up near the main elevator, probably the fourth guard, she guessed. Then hers and the one locked inside the holding cell. Her fingers flew across the keyboard to implement a shutdown of most systems. She knew the security protocols since she'd written them.

She stood when she finished, her gaze still on the image of the cyborg who stood in chains, his eyes closed. He appeared to be sleeping on his feet or perhaps he was in some sort of shutdown cycle. She hoped that wasn't the case. He needed to be alert and ready to flee when she reached him. She headed for the door, kept a mental countdown as she opened it into the hallway, and turned in the direction of the holding cell. She felt down the front of her shirt to locate the small objects she'd smuggled past security, hidden under her breasts inside her bra.

"Crazy," she muttered softly. "I'm going to get killed and it's your fault, Russell."

The lights suddenly cut out around her and she figured the guards would give it about a minute before they grew alarmed. At that point they'd attempt to start lockdown procedure but would then realize she'd cut off all outside communications by jamming them. She jerked open the door to the cell she'd opened from the terminal before she'd restricted the power grid to the entire building. The emergency lights she'd programmed to stay on inside his cell worked. She could see him clearly enough to make out that his eyes were open and fixed on her.

"I don't have time to explain a lot to you." She spoke quickly. "I'm here to get you out. You need to do as I say, stay on my ass, and not pull any shit." She gripped the shackle on his wrist, inserted the small lock pick, and had it open in seconds. "We have about three minutes before they come here to check on you but we need to be long gone by then."

He grabbed her throat the second she freed his hand. Shock tore through Charlie when he forced her head up. She couldn't breathe from his tight hold. He glowered at her in the dim light when their gazes met.

"I know a trap when I see one. Is this a test, human? I am not stupid."

His unusually deep, husky voice startled her for a few heartbeats but then she gripped his fingers. She jerked on them while she struggled to get air into her starving lungs. His hold loosened just enough for her to breathe again. She drew in another breath and then spoke one word.

16

"Council."

His fingers loosened more. "What did you say?"

"The council hired my brother to break you out of here. That is supposed to mean something to you. We could stand here talking but all you're doing is wasting time we don't have. You'll get us both killed."

He released her as quickly as he'd grabbed her. "Do it."

She pushed down her anger over his attack and instead freed his other limbs quickly. She watched him roll his massive, muscled shoulders as he stepped away from the wall before he glared at her again. She decided his soft, dusky-gray skin looked better here than on the monitors. It was such a pretty silvery gray. The sweat beads on his skin even made him a little shiny. She guessed he'd been fighting the chains to have earned the signs of some sort of workout.

"The council really sent you? This isn't a test by humans to see what I will do?"

"No test. We're in danger so could you please shut up and follow me?" She spun away. "Don't talk. Just stick close and stay on my ass. We need to book out of here."

She ran across the room to make up precious seconds they didn't have that had been wasted when he'd grabbed her. She stepped through the door to his cell, into the hallway. She figured he'd either follow her or he wouldn't. Either way she had to leave the building quickly, knowing the guards would arrest her or even kill her. The second object she carried— her tiny flashlight—clicked on and its small beam of light gave her the ability to see a few feet in front of her boots.

"Where are we—"

She twisted around quickly, only to slam face first into a wall of hot, muscular chest. She jerked her head up to stare at his chin. "Shut up. We have to get out of here. Seconds count. Just do what I say. Got it? If you're so damn smart, you should know we're in deep shit. In about two minutes security guards are going to regain control of the systems, lock the building down, and if we're still inside, you should be able to guess how bad that will be for both of us." She turned away from his big body and took off at a jog toward the maintenance elevator to make up for lost time.

It opened as they approached, as she'd programmed it to do. She pointed at the suits that lay on the floor. She'd put them there on her way to her post.

"Get dressed fast. That's the biggest size they had so make do as best you can. We're going to be visible to the police security cameras. We don't want to draw their attention. They'll assume we're just employees exiting the building as long as they don't get a good look at you."

She pushed the button to close the doors and turned to grab the other suit. Frustration filled her when the cyborg just stared at her. He wasn't doing as she'd instructed. She shoved on the coveralls-type suit with jerky motions.

"You're nearly naked, as big as a tree, and distinctive. Cover up or we're never going to make it. Are you deaf? Dress now. It's not going to fit properly and you're far taller than I guessed you'd be so you're going to have to hunch down a bit. Move, damn it. Don't just stand there."

Anger was an easy emotion to read on his strangely handsome features while he glared down at her but then he bent to grab the suit with one hand. She didn't care if she made him angry as long as he covered his body. She zipped the front of her suit closed and reached for the helmet. The lift stopped but the doors didn't open.

"Hurry up!"

"I don't take orders. I give them."

"Bitch about it later. Let's get out of here first."

He had dressed but the suit stretched taut over his freakishly large body. The pants didn't reach his ankles and they gave him a wedgie. She smirked when she glanced at him and saw the material bunched tightly up his ass. Charlie really hoped it felt as uncomfortable as it looked. She didn't like him one bit after he'd squeezed her throat. As soon as he put the helmet on, which effectively covered him from the neck up, she pushed the button to open the doors.

"The camera won't see your feet. Chin up and walk slowly." An alarm sounded throughout the building the second the doors completely opened. She raised her voice. "Just follow my lead."

Charlie strolled down the hallway to the back door and shoved it open. She'd implemented the fire alarms to go off when the elevator doors parted. Every exterior door automatically unlocked to allow them access to the area behind the building. She moved toward the alley next door to put them out of camera range, glanced back at the cyborg, and prayed he didn't weigh as much as she now estimated. She gritted her teeth and had to rethink her plan. The alarm grew silent inside the building.

"Are you as strong as you look? I didn't think you'd be so big when I planned this."

"I'm very strong," he confirmed, his dark-brown gaze narrowing with suspicion.

"Good. Move over here and put this harness on."

He hesitated. She grabbed the leather straps and snapped them around his waist. He tried to take a step back but Charlie gripped the front of his suit with a fist.

"Hold still. I planned to have you wrap around me but no way can I do that. You weigh at least a hundred pounds more than I thought you would. The cable will hold the extra weight but it's a long way up. I'd never be able to hold on to you for that long."

He tilted his head up to stare toward the roof of the building. "Why there?"

"We don't have time to discuss this. The security guards have realized by now that you're gone and patrols will hit the streets. The last place they will look is way up there. Now, do you want to argue over this until we're arrested or do you want to get to safety first?"

He growled a word she didn't catch but he finished harnessing the straps. She bent, removed the small control from her shoe, and then straightened. "Grab me and hold on tight. If you drop me, you won't get outside the city. You need me."

He stared down at her, his eyes still narrowed with suspicion, while his mind obviously worked to ponder his options. Charlie's opinion of him lowered even more. She clenched her teeth and then opened her mouth.

"Look, asshole. I don't like you, you obviously don't like me, but we're in this mess together. If you leave me here to be arrested, you will never make it outside the city or off the planet. I know the escape route and I'm the only chance you've got to reach the council. Stop stalling, quit being a moron, grab me, and let's get the hell out of here before they show up."

He actually growled and Charlie gasped when the cyborg lunged at her. Two massive arms wrapped around her middle, yanked her against his rock-hard body, and mashed her against his suit. She nearly dropped the remote but even if she couldn't see with her face smashed against him, she could hit the button by feel.

Pain crushed around her waist from his strong hold when their feet left the ground and the pulley picked up momentum. The rapid ride made her feel sick and not being able to see only made it worse. Fear gripped her when she slipped an inch down his body. Panicked, she clutched the remote and wrapped her arm around the back of his neck as her leg entwined around the back of his thigh. If he dropped her, she'd plummet to her death on the alley floor. Her brother would have gotten her killed and she didn't want that to happen, out of spite alone.

It seemed like forever, but in reality, Charlie knew it only took about fifteen seconds to reach the roof of the building. She said a silent prayer of thanks when the winch slowed as it had been programmed to do and then they hovered for a second before being swung to the left a few feet. The cyborg's hold on her tightened painfully when he cursed under his breath after his body bumped into something hard enough that she felt it too. He struggled to stand upright when the motion stopped.

Charlie would have landed on her ass on the rooftop if it weren't for her hold on him when he released her as quickly as he'd grabbed her. She jerked her head up now that she wasn't crushed against his chest, shot him a silent promising look of retribution, and unwound her limbs to stand.

"Asshole."

He glowered at her in the dim light. She backed up to give him a once-over. Because she'd thought he'd be shorter, his feet had dragged along the roof floor when they'd been pulled away from the edge of the building. She could see where it happened since there were two faint wet lines from the side of the roof to where he stood. She bent to get a closer look and realized he'd gotten hurt.

"Blood?" She straightened, shocked by the fact that he had organic tissue at all. "How bad is it?"

"My heels dragged and it abraded the skin." He started to tear at the harness to free his big body. "I'll survive and I can walk."

Charlie should have felt terrible for the miscalculation, but then again, he wasn't exactly nice to her. She'd never imagined a cyborg to be so tall. Android work units stood less than six feet high and she'd just assumed he would be about the same height since both had been created by the government. She shrugged it off and turned to head toward the center of the building and hoped he'd follow. For a cyborg, he seemed pretty dense to her. She'd assumed he'd be as smart as a computer.

She halted by the elevator shaft to tear her helmet off and tossed it into the open air vent. She'd previously removed the cover in preparation for their escape. She turned, nearly bumped into the annoying male, and

22

peered up at him. She had to give him points for following but she didn't enjoy how he hovered so close to her body.

"Strip and toss it all inside this vent. We need to change into street clothes."

She gave him her back and half expected him to delay them more with questions but instead an arm extended next to her to drop his discarded helmet down the shaft. She blew out a relieved breath, bent to tear her suit down her legs, and had to struggle to get the pants over her boots.

One glance at her watch assured her they were making good time. If she could keep the tight schedule, they just might make it. She heard sirens blare far below them from the street and her heart accelerated with fear. She knew an army of security guards and civilian police would be closing in around the area to search the grounds. They were safe where they were unless someone had spotted them as they lifted to the roof. If someone had called in a report of that, they would have company in mere minutes.

Charlie dropped her suit down the shaft and turned to point out the bag of clothes. She'd gotten stretch materials and hoped some of it would fit. She faced him and her mouth dropped open as she gawked at the cyborg who straightened to his full height just feet from her.

His chest and muscular arms had impressed her but the sight of the fully naked, gray-skinned male left her speechless. He'd not only removed the suit but those loose shorts the lab had put him in as well. Her gaze lowered and she swallowed hard.

"What? Haven't you ever seen a male without clothing before? You said to remove it all." His deep voice nearly pulled her from her shock.

23

She blinked and knew she'd been caught gaping at the area just below his trim waist. Words still didn't form inside her head. He was aroused, large all over, and the skin of his cock appeared darker than the rest of his body. He didn't have any body hair except for his shoulder-length, wavy, dark-brown hair.

"Female?" He snarled the word.

Her head jerked up and she swallowed the lump that had formed in her throat as she met his gaze. "Why are you hard?"

He frowned. "Adrenaline."

"Right. Whatever." She forced her gaze to look away from the scary sight of just how big adrenaline made him and quickly pointed. "There are clothes inside that bag for you. Put something on." She spun away to give him her back again.

She could hear him move and the slight noise of the bag being unzipped even over the sound of sirens from far below. She took slow, even breaths. For a silvery-gray guy—a cyborg—he had the best body she'd ever seen. The fact that he had been created size proportioned all over burned into her brain. It was a sight she doubted she'd ever forget.

He isn't an asshole. He's a big dick. She couldn't hold back the chuckle or the smirk.

"You find our situation humorous?" He didn't sound amused, judging by the tone of his deep, rumbling voice.

Charlie turned her head to stare at a beefy, muscular ass, bent over while he jerked up the pants he'd removed from the bag. It had to be the

24

best one she'd ever seen. She studied it, grinning. "Let's just say I'm finding my sense of humor."

He turned his head and his dark gaze narrowed dangerously as he glowered at her. "Humans are not rational."

And cyborgs have nice asses, she silently decided, admiring the view once more before she looked away. "Hurry up."

Chapter Two

Charlie glanced at her watch. Sweat started to form on her brow and worry hit her hard. The next phase of their escape would be the most dangerous part of her plan. The cyborg drew her attention when he sighed.

"They do not fit well but I am dressed."

She had to hold back a laugh when she turned his way to see how he looked in street clothes. The shirt stretched tight over his thick, beefy upper body. It reminded her of some of the off-duty guards who frequented the local bar. They dressed that way to purposely show off their muscled arms and abs, trying to pick up sex partners. Her attention lowered and her eyebrows shot up. She couldn't miss seeing the clearly defined, impressive bulge revealed at his crotch. She changed her mind about the appearance he gave in street clothes. He reminded her of one of the drug-addicted male hookers who hung outside the clubs in her old neighborhood who displayed their cocks in thin, tight pants to entice business.

"I said they do not fit me well."

"I heard you." She forced her gaze to lower the rest of the way down his body. "The boots at least fit and hide the fact the pants probably don't reach your ankles. I was able to get hold of a pair of tester boots."

"What are those?"

"They are designed to form to any foot then give a detailed size to the machines the traveling boot maker uses for rich people who enjoy having shit made just for them. I kind of borrowed that pair from my next-door neighbor who does that for a living."

"Even in clothing, I am still unique in appearance. It won't work if your plan is to walk us through any inhabited areas."

Irritation flared. "Really? You don't think they'd notice you're as big as a pillar and gray?"

"Your sarcasm is noted and not welcome at this moment."

"I can't believe anyone is willing to pay so much money to save you." She paused. "I'm Charlie, by the way. What's your name?"

He just stared at her. She inched closer to study his strong bone structure. He appeared human despite his coloring, a very handsome one at that, with his strong jawline, straight, perfect nose, and generous, full lips. Dark, thick eyelashes fringed his beautiful eyes but his silvery-gray complexion set him apart more than his attractiveness.

"I'm saving your ass, cyborg. Did you know those lab jerks were planning to do an autopsy on you? Do you need a clue what that means? They were going to cut you up to examine you a tiny piece at a time and they are such assholes that I'm not sure they would have even bothered to kill you before they started. I asked your name."

He leaned closer, anger darkened his features slightly, and she had to acknowledge that he did intimidation really well as he scowled at her from his height. She stood her ground, refusing to retreat even an inch while she glared back at him. She'd dealt with many bullies in her lifetime, and while he definitely had to be the most frightening one she'd ever come across, hands down, she knew the only way to handle him would be to stick up for herself.

"Don't anger me. Get me out of here and off this planet now."

Her eyebrows arched while she gaped at him. "You don't give me orders. We can fight each other every step of the way or you can start doing what I say. Maybe they scrambled your circuits or screwed up your programming when they had you locked up so reboot your systems until you take orders better. Give me your name or tell me how to address you. Were you assigned numbers? I know a lot of the work androids go by them."

His mouth curved downward more and small lines appeared next to his eyes. "I don't take orders from humans and I'm as sentient as you are."

"Great. So you really are just an asshole. Fine." She turned away from him, hoped he wouldn't attack, and stormed across the rooftop toward the air conditioning shed on the far side of the building. "I'm getting the hell out of here. You can come with me or wait around to be returned to your holding cell. Have fun with your autopsy if you stay."

His boots made a slight noise when he followed her. She headed to the smaller of the two storage sheds on the roof and jerked open the door. She hesitated and then glanced back at the cyborg to see his reaction. He looked perplexed as he peered at the vehicle she'd parked there before he met her gaze.

"You look a bit confused. Haven't you ever seen an air cyclone before? I...um...borrowed it too. I hope you're not afraid of heights."

"I don't know what it is and I'm not intolerant of high places."

28

"Oh goodie," she snorted. She lifted her leg and straddled the seat. "It's got thrusters and it will hover about ten feet from any solid surface."

"We're on top of a building. This is a useless piece of machinery if you hoped we'd escape on it, unless you plan to take the elevator down to the first floor of the building. Is that a possibility without detection?"

"We could try that but I'm pretty certain even if we managed to make it out of the ground floor lobby, we wouldn't make it half a block down the street before we were captured." She forced a smile. "You're going to have to trust me, cyborg. Please get on the back and hold on to me tightly."

He didn't move. "There is nowhere to drive that machine."

One glance at her watch sent fear inching up Charlie's spine. She met his gaze. "We're going to be found if you don't shut up, trust me, and get on the back of this thing now."

"There is no reasonable—"

"I'm as dead as you'll be if we are arrested," she interrupted. "Get on the damn seat behind me, stop arguing, and trust me. I don't have time to talk you through my escape plan. We're behind schedule and they will search every building, floor by floor. I don't want to be here when they reach the roof. Please? Get on!"

"It makes no sense." He actually straddled the seat of the cyclone, behind her. "Of course logically I see your point. If I were in charge of a hunt for fugitives I would check every inch of all buildings." He hesitated before his two big hands encircled her hips to grip them firmly. "What is it you have in mind?"

29

She flipped the "on" switch. "Hang on and don't be alarmed in a second when the auto belts wrap around your thighs to keep you in place." She started the engine by gripping the steering bars. "Put your feet on top of the running boards."

The cyclone lifted a few inches then hummed softly while levitating above the floor. Charlie put her feet flat in front of where she'd told him to put his and as soon as she felt the secure press of the auto belts over her thighs, she pushed forward. The vehicle slowly accelerated out of the shed to the open roof.

"What is your strategy for escaping the roof?"

"All you need to know is, don't freak out."

"What does that mean?"

"Just close your eyes and know I tested this first. We'll be fine," Charlie assured him.

"What—"

She said a silent prayer, pressed her thumb down firmly on the energy button, and gunned the engine. The cyclone shot forward, increasing speed and height as she aimed it toward the edge of the roof. They went sailing over the twenty foot gap between the buildings.

Pain made her clench her teeth when the cyborg squeezed her hips in a near-crushing clench. The cyclone stabilizers took over to prevent them from crashing into the rooftop of the next building. They bounced a little on the air cushion the thrusters gave them when the sensors made contact with the solid surface, a sick feeling churned inside her stomach, but she didn't ease up on the power button. She kept it full throttle, ignored the bruising hold he kept on her, and aimed for the next roof. They sailed over another gap. By the fifth building jump, he seemed to realize they weren't going to crash or fly off a building to plummet to their deaths.

"You're insane," he raged but he eased his hold somewhat.

She didn't say a word, unable to really fault him for his thoughts, and braced for another jump. Three blocks later she finally stopped the cyclone and killed the engine. Her heart still pounded from the fear but they'd made it. The cyclone gently lowered to the roof until it settled firmly onto the flat surface.

"That wasn't so bad."

The cyborg yanked his hands off her the second the belts released their thighs. His big body lurched away from the cyclone. He took a few shaky steps before he whipped around to scowl at her. Rage darkened his features and his hands fisted at his sides when he growled, "You could have killed us."

Charlie released the handle grips and stood on weak knees after she eased off the seat. "No, the government security officers or the civilian police would have done that if they'd caught us. Make yourself useful and grab that tarp behind you. Cover the cycle so it's harder to spot. We have a shuttle to get you to before they expand the search and lock down the entire city."

"They should have sent a male to break me out. Women on this planet obviously are still as irrational and irresponsible as ever."

Anger rose instantly inside Charlie. She'd risked her neck to get him out of the cell, saved his life in the process, and he had the nerve to insult

31

her. "Do you see a guy standing before you? No, you don't. Guess what? Nobody else was irrational or irresponsible enough to take on the government to save your big, gray ass. You should drop to your knees before me and show some gratitude."

He growled again and took a threatening step closer before he halted. "I am no longer forced to perform sexual acts upon your females."

Shock overwhelmed her when his words sank into her stunned brain. An image of him on his knees in that context stole her breath away. The guy had definite sex appeal that made her wonder what it would be like to have him touch her. She'd once been assigned the task of fixing a male sex droid with a malfunctioning "off" switch. The thing had used his hands to massage her breasts, despite her protests, the entire time she'd had his chest open to replace the fried circuits that kept him from shutting down. She'd hated the way her body had gotten turned on but she had to admit the thing knew how to touch a woman to make her ache. She'd bet cyborgs were more advanced than androids and wondered how complex his sexual programming would be. That thought was quickly replaced by another one that made her grimace.

"Ewww. They made you do Doctor Correl? She's like a hundred years old." Her gaze raked up and down him. "Did you break her?"

"That hag who drew my blood this morning?" Danger radiated off him as he took another step closer. "I spoke of my captivity before I escaped Earth."

She released the breath she'd held. "Oh." She suddenly laughed. "That's good."

"Good?" He snarled, advancing again until he towered over her—at least a full foot taller, which put him at about six feet four. He was so close, she could feel his body heat.

"I didn't mean it was good that you once were programmed to do that stuff but I am relieved you didn't have to touch Doctor Correl. Not only is she older than a century but she's meaner than an attack droid."

Their gazes held while she watched him battle his anger. She realized they were wasting time by having a glaring contest and decided to try to defuse the situation. They had enough people out to get them at that moment without turning on each other.

"Chill out, cyborg. I didn't mean that you should open my pants. I meant that you should be saying 'thank you' for getting you out of that place before they strapped you down and started examining you with sharp, pointy knives. You know—grovel, not, well...you know."

He eased back more. "You weren't implying that I should use my mouth to stroke you to climax as payment for you releasing me from being a prisoner?"

His blunt words left her speechless. A mental image of him doing just that made her back up, bump the cyclone, and she nearly tripped. She shook her head while she found her footing.

He spun away and grabbed the tarp. "Understood. I am grateful for the rescue but I do not appreciate the implementation of it. A male would have come up with a better plan that involved less danger." He bent, showed off his beefy ass molded inside the tight pants, and then approached her. "I'm valuable and you took too many risks with my life."

Charlie moved out of his way to give him room to toss the cover over the vehicle. "You're something all right." She headed for the stairwell of the building. "Outdated, a chauvinist, and an asshole," she muttered.

"My hearing is enhanced." He sounded pissed. "I heard you."

"How is your night vision?" She lifted her hand and flipped her middle finger up at him, over her shoulder. "Move it, Mr. Valuable Cyborg."

He growled behind her. She itched to get her hands on his access panel and remove that little annoying quirk from his programming. The building door remained unlocked, the way she'd left it, to allow them to enter the stairwell. She begun praying they didn't run into anyone. People didn't really use stairs anymore but they remained intact inside older buildings. Unless the power failed or a fire broke out to force other people into the stairwell, she estimated they'd make it to the basement undetected.

His heavy tread remained behind her so she knew he followed. At the basement level she faced him. "Wait here."

"You're not leaving me behind."

"I'm making sure no one is within sight when you step out. I have a hovercraft parked two stalls over. We're going to drive out of here but I can't risk anyone seeing you. There aren't cameras inside this building. It's why I picked it."

He nodded curtly. She paused. "What's your name?"

He hesitated. "I am Zorus."

"What kind of name is that?"

34

"It's a masculine name intended to be used for a male. We have that in common."

Her eyebrows arched. "Zing on the insult I haven't heard a thousand times before. I meant what culture did it come from? I've never heard it before."

He hesitated again. It was obvious that he didn't want to answer. "It's one I gave myself. It has meaning to me."

Her curiosity was pricked. "What's the meaning?"

He said nothing.

"You want out of here?" She decided to be a bitch. He totally deserved it. "It's the least you could tell me since I've risked my life saving you."

Irritation showed clearly on his handsome features. "It stands for zestful of rights undermining supremacy."

Charlie gaped at him. "Uh-huh. Okay."

"You were never deemed subhuman and under the total control of others. I was young and newly freed when I came up with the words that formed the acronym of my name. Forus sounded wrong to me. The E would have stood for enthusiastic." He gave her a cold look that would freeze water. "What is the meaning of zing?"

"Forget it. It's slang, which I suppose you weren't programmed to speak."

"Why do you have a male's name?" His dark gaze lowered down her body slowly. "Are you really just a small male with a female voice?"

"You know," she warned softly, "if I didn't need to deliver you completely undamaged to get paid enough money to escape Earth Government, I just might turn you into a toaster or something." Anger burned inside her at his calculated insult. She knew she wasn't gorgeous but nobody had ever implied she might not really be a woman. "My parents had me during the years of the black flu."

"I'm familiar with that bit of your history. We occasionally monitor what happens on Earth to assess their danger level. The black flu struck mostly human females with a death rate of the infected estimated at seventy percent. Earth Government implemented a quarantine until the epidemic could be contained. The affected sections were deemed irrelevant. Why would that have any relevance on your given name?"

The urge to deck the big bastard had her fighting hard to keep a lid on her temper. "I was one of those irrelevant people who lived in one of the poor sections nobody gave a shit about. I lost an older sister, my grandmother, and two aunts when it spread through the neighborhood. They were all denied medical attention. The only intervention the government decided to give was to snatch healthy, newborn baby girls to be given away to some high-ranking officials who wanted to adopt them. Or they donated us to be medical experiments. My parents gave me a boy's name and a sympathetic doctor put 'male' on my birth registration to protect me from either of those fates."

Something in his features softened. "You're irrelevant."

Charlie spun away, gripped the door, and jerked it open hard enough to flinch when a muscle inside her arm protested. *Think of the money and don't kill the bastard*, she thought, fuming over his insult. She took a few deep breaths in an attempt to calm down before she forced herself to study the parking basement. Nothing moved.

"Come on," she called softly. "Let's get you onto that shuttle."

She jogged toward the hovercraft at a brisk pace. The sooner she dropped him off, the faster she got paid and could get the hell away from him. When she saw her brother again, she would kick his ass for getting her into this mess and subjecting her to the conceited, rude cyborg.

She squeezed into her seat and pushed a button to open the passenger door since he wasn't coded to automatically access her vehicle. The sight of his large, tall frame folded into the small seat made her smirk. His knees were shoved against the dash and he had to tuck his chin to his chest to fit inside the compartment. He looked uncomfortable and she could have sworn he flinched when the door closed, probably hitting his hip and thigh area.

"My irrelevant ass is taking you to safety so remember that when you blast away from the surface of Earth on your way back to wherever the hell you came from."

He turned his head just enough to see her. "I meant no insult by that term. I meant we have that in common as well." His deep voice softened. "Cyborgs and grunts were assigned the same insignificant classification by the government. We were both deemed a disposable workforce."

She stared into his brown eyes, saw no cruelty there, and relaxed as her anger faded. "Oh."

"That is a compliment that we have things in common."

37

Charlie wasn't so sure of that assessment since the cyborg wasn't someone she liked very much. "Let's get you to safety. No one can see inside here with the tinted glass." She started the engine and pulled away the parking space. "We're only a few miles from the port located just outside the city limits." She forced her focus on where she steered. *Maybe I was too hard on him. The stress he's been under since his capture has to be over the top. I'd be a bit grumpy too.* "And I'm definitely female."

"I knew that. I wished to insult you and it worked. I hate humans and female ones are worse than the males, in my opinion."

So much for him not being a total asshole. "My opinion of you isn't real high either, Zorus." His name sounded strange when she said it. "Why don't you shut up and let me drive? I had to disconnect the onboard computer that usually does the piloting since it would have reported you to the authorities if they put a search bulletin out with your description. It's coded in all vehicles to lock the doors, shut down, and alert the police if it realizes we're the ones being sought. I didn't have time to hack into the mainframe to disable the auto systems."

"You should allow me to control the vehicle. I'm still appalled over your cyclone piloting skills."

Charlie clenched her teeth, flipped off the stabilizers, and drove faster, swerving as often as possible. She smiled when he softly cursed every time his knees and head repeatedly bumped against the interior as she slammed him around.

"Sorry about that," she lied, going just a little faster to give him a rougher ride.

"You are doing this on purpose."

She refused to glance his way. They drove until they reached the freight port of the manufacturing area outside the city. After dark nothing moved on the street, the human employees had already clocked out for the day, leaving their jobs to the automated systems. She parked and finally gave him her full attention.

"The android work shift has started. They only register life forms so they won't notice your skin color. You won't draw their attention unless you say or do something odd. Just stay on my ass and don't speak. Do you think you can handle that?"

"Yes." He peered through the windshield at the shipyard. "I'm leaving on a cargo ship?"

"I'm sorry but first class seats inside one of those luxury liners happened to be booked solid and, oh yeah, people would scream and totally panic if they got an eyeful of a cyborg. According to the government, your kind murdered humans on sight after you fried the circuits that kept you under their control. People pretty much think cyborgs were killing machines taking out anything within sight."

"I was not lodging a complaint. That is also untrue. We only took out the humans we had to kill during our escape." His gaze narrowed. "You are unpleasant with your sarcasm."

"You're not a joy to be around either." Charlie shoved open the door and exited the vehicle. She resisted the urge to watch the cyborg get out of the car, figuring it wouldn't be easy for him, but would amuse her. "Hurry up," she ordered.

He met her at the front of the car. She scanned the area, not seeing any movement. Her heart raced from fear but she also felt relieved they'd made it that far without being arrested. That actually surprised her. She's been half sure this mission would be suicide. She assumed he followed as she kept in the shadows of the buildings to head for the docking area where the shuttle should be waiting.

She froze in place when a door suddenly opened. Ten feet in front of them light poured out onto the dark pavement and boots struck concrete. Charlie watched with dread as the guy exited the building and knew if he turned his head there would be no missing the sight of Zorus. They had nowhere to hide, nothing to crouch behind, so she moved on instinct.

The guy didn't see her until she rounded him to keep his attention on her instead of behind him where she'd come from. Her hands rubbed her hips and she directed her sweetest smile at him.

"Hi."

The man wore the uniform of a dock supervisor. Surprise lifted his eyebrows but his green gaze roamed from her face down to her boots. "This is a restricted area. I'm going to have to notify security." He reached for the communicator strapped to his wrist.

Charlie grabbed his arm, careful not to seem too aggressive. "I just came looking for some food." She used her other hand to motion Zorus to move around the building out of sight. "That's all. Please don't call security. I've got a few credits to pay you if you just look the other way. Sometimes the auto loaders drop a package of rations, they break open, and you guys just toss them into your trash disposers. I sneaked in to grab a few for my family before they are incinerated. Please have a heart and don't turn me in for raiding your garbage."

Movement from the corner of her eye assured her that Zorus followed her silent order to ease around the building out of sight. Once she bribed the worker, she could meet him there and get him to the shuttle. As soon as she got paid, she'd head for the official space port to meet her brother. Russell's contacts, who'd ordered the rescue mission, had arranged passage on one of the coach liners heading for Saturn where their new lives would begin. She tried not to wince over the idea of living inside biodomes for the rest of her life, breathing recycled air.

The guy hesitated and Charlie knew she had him. No one in their right mind would pass up a bribe over trash. If she were trying to steal the good stuff, then no way would he take it for fear of losing his job, but it wouldn't be any skin off his nose if she wanted the stuff they destroyed. She eased her hand inside her pocket, released his arm, and pulled out some credits. She held them up.

"Thank you."

He grabbed her hand instead of the money, twisted her wrist painfully, and knocked her off balance enough to spin her around. She cried out as her body left the ground when his other arm wrapped around her waist, and after a few long strides, he slammed her into a tall crate that acted as a wall for him.

"I won't turn you in but I don't want money," he panted.

Pain stunned her where her forehead had struck the unforgiving surface. He hoisted her higher to push against her body with his and a knee slammed between her thighs to pin her so he could free his hands. He tore at the back of her pants. It sank into her dazed mind quickly that he planned to rape her.

Heavy breathing fanned across her skin when he tore her shirt with his other hand to bare her shoulder. That action and the rough tug on her waist shook her enough to push back the pain and react. She slammed her elbow into the guy's ribs and threw her head back in the same action. More pain stabbed through her brain, this time coming from her skull when it met his jaw, but it worked. His hold loosened and he staggered away enough for her to drop to the ground.

"You perverted prick," she hissed, twisting to face her attacker.

A hand wrapped around her throat, revealing that his years of dock work had made him strong enough to easily yank her off the ground. Pure panic gripped Charlie. She clawed at the arm attached to the fingers choking her. She kicked at him but he seemed immune to the blows or her nails digging into his skin. He kept her dangling from the ground and unable to breathe with his fingers wrapped around her neck.

"You're going to love what I do to you," the man cursed. "Stop clawing me, you little bitch." He gave her a shake.

"Actually," a deep voice suddenly stated softly, "she doesn't appear to enjoy your handling in the least."

The dock worker released Charlie, dropped her onto her feet, and rotated to face who'd spoken. Zorus punched him in the face before her attacker could get a look at him. The sound of breaking bone made Charlie inwardly wince while she rubbed her throat, choked a little, but forced air inside her starved lungs. She watched when Zorus bent over the fallen man, grabbed his neck, and with one more horrible sound of bone breaking, released the lifeless body.

"You didn't have to kill him," she rasped. "But thank you."

Zorus straightened to shoot her an icy glare. "I have no tolerance for a rapist who interferes with my escape."

She stared up at him, a chill going down her spine. "Are you going to have no tolerance for me when I'm no longer useful?"

"I have no plans to kill you."

She pulled her frayed emotions together, dropped her hand from her sore throat, and nodded curtly. "Good. I'd like to survive my first, and hopefully last, venture into doing something this dangerous."

"I take it you usually steal items that aren't such a priority as I must be."

"I'm not a thief if that's what you're implying." She refused to glance down at the dead body near her boots. She headed for the building, certain Zorus followed. "I'm just a programmer who happened to land a job at that facility you were kept in. I ran their security systems until my brother volunteered me to break you out of there. Now I'm going to be a fugitive from Earth Government." She paused long enough to peer around the corner. She moved when the coast looked clear. "We have being wanted by the government in common now too."

A hot hand clamped down on top of her bare skin along the curve of her shoulder. It startled her. She swiveled her head to stare up at the cyborg when his gentle hold brought her to a halt.

43

"You're bleeding. He scratched your skin but its minor." His fingers released her. "Why didn't your brother free me? I can't understand why he would send you on such a dangerous mission. Males are protective of female relatives."

"You haven't met my brother." She turned her gaze forward to scan the area again. "There was money involved and he didn't care how risky it might be for me as long as the price was right. He'd never endanger his own neck for anything. He's got me for that." She realized the bitterness probably wasn't hidden in her tone but she didn't care. Zorus had saved her from a bad fate, she still felt shaken at how close she'd come to being sexually assaulted, and she doubted she'd have been able to get away on her own. "Let's go. I don't see anyone and this is our building. Stay close. You're almost to safety."

Chapter Three

Charlie tried to hide her terror when they faced the men inside. They looked pretty badass, the types she'd grown up with in the wrong side of classification. They might as well have worn signs stating they were vicious criminals. She kept her body between them and the silent Zorus behind her.

"Captain Varel?" She tried to sound fearless and just hoped it worked.

A blond, tall man who looked to be in his forties stepped forward. His piercing green eyes met hers and his blood-chilling smile made her want to whimper. "You made good time."

"Thanks." She cleared her throat. "As you can see, I brought the cyborg to be returned to where he came from."

The guy flicked a glance at the cyborg, nodded, and then turned to one of his men. "Go get her payment." He faced forward and addressed Zorus directly after his man left the building quickly.

"Your cyborg council hired me to rescue you. Councilman Coval sends his regards. We will transport you to the edge of the solar system where another ship will meet us for your transfer." The captain bowed. "I'm Barney Varel, the captain of the *Cutter*, and it's a pleasure to meet you, Councilman Zorus."

Charlie could tell Zorus wasn't happy when he frowned. "Why didn't they collect me?"

"The council didn't want to be too close to Earth, for obvious reasons." Captain Varel kept the frosty smile in place. "My business is transporting things away from Earth safely. No one searches my shuttle. I'm the best at what I do and today that's getting you the hell off the surface."

"Understood." Zorus crossed his arms. "I am ready to leave."

"If you'll come with me." The captain waved his hand toward the shuttle parked outside the open back cargo door. "We have clothing that will fit you and food waiting. I also have a doctor onboard if you need medical assistance. Your health and welfare are my main concern."

Charlie reached out and gripped the cyborg's arm. "He doesn't leave my side until I get paid. That was the agreement. You're supposed to contact the trustee and have it transferred to me."

She half expected Zorus to argue but he didn't pull away, something he could have easily done. Sweat beaded her brow and she feared something would go wrong. She wasn't stupid enough to blindly trust a career criminal to keep his word. It was his business to prey on the weak and screw over anyone he could. She tried not to think about her ex-boyfriend, who would have to complete the deal.

Boots sounded from the docked shuttle and Charlie gasped when her brother and three other men entered the building. Russell should have been waiting for her to meet him on the passenger shuttle at the space port. He waved at her and didn't look injured.

"Hi, baby sis."

"What are you doing here?" Her fingers tightened on Zorus.

"Change of plans." Russell stopped a good ten feet from her. He held an electronic pad under his arm. "They paid us for the cyborg."

Someone suddenly grabbed Charlie from behind to tear her away from Zorus and hauled her off her feet. A sharp jab in her arm instantly had her crying out in pain and then a weird sensation quickly spread throughout her body that made her lightheaded and dizzy. She tried to struggle but her limbs didn't respond. She hung limply in someone's hold.

"What is going on?" Zorus moved in front of her. "Release her immediately."

"I'm her brother." Russell came forward. "It's all cool. Nobody is going to hurt her. I just knew she wasn't going to take this well and asked these guys to sedate her a little. My baby sis has a hell of a temper along with a mean right hook."

"What did you do?" Charlie's voice sounded strange and her lips were numb but she managed the ability to lift her gaze to stare at her brother.

Russell moved closer to peer at her face. "It's nothing you're thinking."

Fear inched up her spine and she managed to turn her attention to Zorus. Fury darkened his features and his hands were fisted at his sides. She looked back at her brother.

"You said he'd be safely taken back to where he came from. I wouldn't have brought him here otherwise."

"He will be."

She didn't believe him. She sent Zorus a terrified plea with her gaze. "Run."

"Hold up, Councilman Zorus," Captain Varel ordered. "You are being returned to your people. I give you my word and I have a vid from your council to prove that. This doesn't involve you at all. This is about her."

47

"What is going on?" Zorus moved closer to Charlie until they nearly touched and he faced Russell. "Why have you drugged her?"

Another thought hit and Charlie gaped at her brother. "You're taking all the money and leaving me here to die, aren't you?" Anger burned next. "I threw my life away to get you out of this mess and you're going to abandon me for the government to find?"

"No!" Russell scoffed. "That's not it at all. I'm taking all the money, sure, but you're leaving too. It's just that you're not going to Saturn with me." He kept his distance as if he feared she'd find the strength to attack him. "It's just that when Gerald realized you'd have to flee Earth with me, well, hell, Charlie. He made me a deal I couldn't refuse."

"Gerald?"

"He still loves you and he wants you to be his mistress."

Charlie gaped at him, too shocked to even find words.

"You kept turning him down when he tried to talk to you about it. He's got a great little place on the moon, a real little love nest, and he promised me he's got the security in place to keep you there for as long as he wants. I know you're going to be really mad at me and it's not what you wanted, but he won't hurt you. It's not as though it will be as bad as a real prison."

Pain gripped her heart and tears blinded her. "You sold me? I'm your sister!"

Russell hesitated. "You used to like him. It won't be so bad. Look on the bright side. No one will find you where he's taking you. You'll be safe from the government."

"Don't do this." Tears slid down her cheeks and she couldn't even wipe them away with her useless arms. "I don't want to be his whore."

"So dramatic." Russell shook his head and turned to the captain. "Gerald's ship will hail you after you leave the system. Keep her drugged until he takes possession of her. She may look small and harmless but don't let it fool you."

Charlie watched Russell turn away from her and walk toward the side doors of the building. The brutal truth that he'd really sold her sank in. "Russell?"

He paused. "It's done, Charlie."

"I'll get free, and when I do, I'll be coming after you." Her threat hung in the air, crystal clear.

He turned his head to stare at her. He paled. "No, you won't. Gerald isn't going to let you go. He assured me there'd be no way for you to escape." He took a deep breath. "He'll kill you before he lets you leave him. He knows you'll never willingly allow him to touch you and you'll want revenge if you ever get free. I'd make him happy if I were you, by pretending you don't mind being his mistress. You'll live longer."

Russell left the building without a backward glance. The stranger who held her adjusted his grip and started to walk away, carrying her. Charlie hung limply in the circle of his arms, only able to move her gaze, which landed on Zorus. He walked beside them but he didn't say a word. More tears slid down her face but she didn't try to talk her way out of the mess her brother had gotten her into. It would be pointless.

49

A hive of activity took place inside the shuttle's cargo area. Four men turned to leer at Charlie but the captain snapped at them to secure the crates along the walls. He ignored Charlie completely.

"By this time tomorrow, you'll be back with your people, Councilman Zorus," the captain assured him.

Zorus said nothing in response to the captain's words, his jaw set in a grim line, and walked in front of the man carrying Charlie. They separated a few turns inside the belly of the ship and she found herself taken inside a bare room that only contained a cot. The man dumped her onto it and then hovered over her.

He had to be in his twenties, blond, and resembled the captain enough for her to guess he had to be his son. "That's a tough break that your own brother fucked you over." He grinned, his gaze traveling down her body. "Too bad you're off limits. I'd love to get my hands on you." He winked before he quit the room. The second the doors closed, the lights shut off to leave her in total darkness.

Hot tears poured down the sides of her face but her arms refused to move to even wipe them away. Her body rested in a twisted position, half on her back and her side, the hard cot uncomfortable, and there wasn't anything she could do but feel helpless and betrayed.

* * * * *

Zorus studied the cramped but clean room he'd been assigned. New clothes were folded neatly on top of the narrow bed and food had been placed on the only table inside the room. He ignored the captain until he'd

50

assessed every inch of the living space. He finally gave his attention to the human. The captain spoke first.

"Do you want a doctor?"

"No." Zorus folded his arms over his chest. "I want the details of the trade agreement for the human female and the male who intends to buy her."

The captain frowned. "I just deliver shit."

"How much did this Gerald pay for her?"

"I have no idea. In this business, I don't ask questions."

The image of Charlie's tear-streaked features weren't something Zorus could forget. She'd saved him from being held prisoner by Earth Government. What bothered him the most had been when she'd realized she'd been double-crossed. She'd ordered him to run. Humans rarely surprised him but she had when she'd tried to warn him when she thought he was in danger.

"Make it your business."

The shorter human shifted his stance. "Why?"

Zorus hesitated and then made a decision. "I owe her a debt. Find out that information and I'll purchase her from the human."

"I don't think so. Gerald Yazer isn't someone who lets go of anything he wants. I got the impression he wants her bad."

"Everything has a price."

"I've had dealings with the guy before and he's a rich, pampered ass." A pair of intelligent eyes studied Zorus closely. "Besides, if you want to buy a woman, I can locate better-looking ones. I have some onboard. I could rent you one if you want sex. I keep her for my personal use. She's beautiful and clean. If you really enjoy her body, I'd be willing to part with her if the price is high enough."

Disgust rose inside Zorus. "That isn't what I want to purchase the human for. I stated that I owe her a debt. What are you being paid to deliver her?"

"Twenty thousand credits."

"I'll pay you a hundred thousand credits to allow her to escape."

"To escape?"

"You heard me."

"You're willing to pay that but you don't plan to keep her?"

"I have no use for a human slave. They cause trouble."

"Then why even bother to waste that many credits?"

"She's rude and annoying, but for a human, she has unique qualities I'd hate to think will be broken when her spirit is. I doubt she'll take to captivity well. The human male will probably kill her quickly because of excessive sarcasm."

"You have that much on you?" The captain's gaze lowered down Zorus. "If you do, I'm not seeing it, and I'm pretty sure, as tight as those clothes are, I would."

"My people will pay you. Just tell them to add it to whatever you're being paid. I have the authority to authorize it."

Green eyes glittered. "I have a reputation you know."

"A hundred thousand is five times more profit than you'd manage if you just delivered the woman. Take it or leave it." Zorus glared at him. "I won't go any higher in price."

"And you want me to give her an opportunity to escape?"

"Yes."

"That would mean giving her access to a life pod. We're ready to lift off and need to do that in the next ten minutes to avoid being searched. If I just have someone carry her off the shuttle she'll be located by the authorities before the drugs wear off."

Zorus contained his irritation. "Fine. I'll agree to a hundred fifty thousand credits. That will more than cover the cost of you losing a pod."

"Deal." Captain Varel grinned. "I'll order my men not to give her another dose of the paralyzing drug and mark up the exits to the nearest pod clear enough that she can't miss them. In about three hours she'll be able to move again and my men will allow her to leave the ship without interfering."

"Make sure there is enough fuel on the pod to allow her to make it safely to Saturn. That is where she planned to go."

"Fine." The captain nodded and turned away. "I'm going to double-check that the funds are available before I allow her escape."

"You do that." Zorus knew the council would agree. "Tell them it's a life debt payment I sanctioned. They'll understand."

The moment the captain left, Zorus reached for the ill-fitting clothing he wore to remove them. He'd repaid Charlie and she seemed to be a resourceful human. She'd sworn vengeance on her brother and he didn't doubt she'd locate the greedy human once she reached Saturn and make him pay for his treachery.

* * * * *

Charlie slowly regained movement in her fingers first and then could stir her wrist. She had no idea how much time had passed but she'd run out of tears. It really hurt that her brother had sold her to Gerald. It shouldn't have surprised her that Russell would do something so low but it had. Family should mean something to him.

Frustration and bitterness swamped her as she wiggled her toes. First she needed to get out of this mess and then she'd hunt down her dear brother, take her share of the money before he gambled it away, and then she planned to start a new life without him. The promise to her parents seemed irrelevant under the circumstances. If they were still alive to see how low Russell had sunk they wouldn't have asked her to look out for him in the first place.

The fact that Gerald played a part in this nightmare didn't surprise her in the least. He'd tossed her over for a rich woman who waved a new life in his face but he'd wanted to keep Charlie on the side. She would never allow him to touch her after he'd ripped her heart to shreds. He wouldn't have resisted an opportunity to get her under his thumb. Anger made her heart pump faster, working the drug out of her system until she managed to move her legs.

It took time but she sat up. The dark room revealed nothing but she remembered where the door was. She stood on unsteady legs and wobbled forward until she touched a metal wall. By feel, she managed to find the door and the panel next to it. Lights blinded her when she found the "on" button for them.

The shuttle had outdated technology, something she felt grateful for as she used her fingernails to pop off the panel. She raised her knee to retrieve the knife she'd stashed inside her boot. The idiots hadn't frisked her for concealed weapons. A smile curved her mouth as she hacked wires then withdrew her small kit from her bra that contained the tools she had used to free Zorus. She worked quickly.

"What is your request?" The computer had a masculine voice.

"Display a layout of the shuttle's interior."

A blueprint of the shuttle appeared on the screen above the panel. It even detailed where she'd been dumped.

"Show me the life signs that aren't crew members."

One room lit up since the computer had been fooled into thinking Charlie had full access. Zorus had been assigned a room on the same level of the three-floor shuttle but his quarters were located on the opposite end, one corridor over.

"Now display all heat signatures."

The crew seemed to mostly be grouped together on the lowest deck in what appeared to be the mess hall. Two signatures showed near the engines but none shared the same level she and Zorus were on. The cyborg's stationary heat signature assured her he wasn't moving around the ship.

"Track me and verbally warn me if anyone attempts to enter this section."

"Confirmed."

"Give me full voice command."

"Confirmed."

"Open the doors."

The doors slid open to reveal a dim hallway. Charlie stepped out, confident that she wouldn't run into anyone, steered right, and used the wall to keep her upright as her still-sluggish legs struggled to carry her forward. She paused in front of the door where Zorus was quartered.

"Open the door."

The second it slid open Zorus whirled to face her, his big body going into a defense posture. She gripped the open doorjamb to stare at him. "Hi. I'm the cavalry so don't attack me. My body is still too messed up and my reflexes are too screwed to block any punches you may throw. Are you all right?"

"I locked the door." His body relaxed but he looked distinctly surprised. "What are you doing here?"

"Saving your ass if you need it." She cleared her throat. "I'm escaping but I wanted to check on you first. If that son of a bitch brother of mine lied to me about our plans then I wasn't sure he really intended for you to be returned to your people. If he set you up too then I sure wasn't going to leave you behind."

Zorus' dark gaze widened. "Why didn't you just escape?"

Charlie frowned at him. "Do you need rescuing or not? I'm sure someone will realize I hacked the computer sooner than later. We need to be off the shuttle before they do. We'll be screwed once they take back control. At the moment, I can get us out of here and disable them long enough for us to put some distance between us and the pod I plan to steal. I'm going to have their computer run diagnostics. It will lock it up for a good twenty minutes with this old shuttle. That will give us plenty of time to make good on our escape."

The big cyborg gaped at her, mute and shocked.

"Time is not our friend now, Zorus. Do you need to come with me or are you cool?"

Her words seemed to shake him. "What if I were in danger?"

"We'll find the nearest space port and I'll hack Into a secure line for you to contact your people to pick you up. I'm heading for Saturn to have a little family reunion once I'm sure you're safe."

"You are truly concerned for my well-being?"

"Duh." She closed her eyes, attempting to fight off a dizzy spell. It took a lot to look at him and remain standing. "We need to go if you want out of here." Her eyes snapped open when the worst of it passed.

"You're pale and shaking."

"I'm drugged still and I feel as though my body weighs four hundred pounds. It's all I can do to stay on my feet. Time is wasting."

"Movement on lift two," the computer voice stated. "It is headed for this level."

Alarm jolted Charlie. "We've got to go, Zorus. Someone is coming. Stay on my ass and I'll get you out of here."

She turned and her knees collapsed from the sudden movement. Pain had her cursing when metal and skin slammed together with only the thin barrier of her pants to cushion her. She ended up crouched on her hands and knees inside the hallway without the ability to push back up to her feet. She hated the weakness that gripped her.

"Go," she called out. "Head left and you can't miss the lift at the end of the corridor. They have two life pods docked in the secondary cargo hold. I'll transfer over control to you to enable you to escape. I'll cycle the diagnostics once you're clear." She gasped in air. "Computer, I—"

"Unbelievable," Zorus muttered as he bent to her and his arm slid around her waist. His other hand griped her shoulder. He lifted her carefully, easily rolled her over into the cradle of his arms, and scowled down at her while he hoisted her against his chest. He straightened to carry her within his strong arms. "You want me to leave you behind?"

"I'll slow you down. Drop me and run, damn it. Save yourself." She stared up into his beautiful eyes. "I'll get away later. There's not much I can't hack."

He didn't move. "I'll keep that in mind for future reference."

He didn't toss her aside to flee. "You have to go, Zorus. Someone is going to be coming any second from the right side of the corridor. Head left toward the other lift."

He carried her back into the sleeping quarters he'd been assigned to and strode to his bunk. The doors closed firmly behind them. Charlie couldn't believe his stupidity. She'd given him a chance to escape but he'd refused. It was a hell of a time for him to find a conscience if that's why he wouldn't leave her behind.

The tall cyborg bent and gently eased her smaller frame down on top of the comfortable mattress. His arms slid out from under her quickly before he straightened. "You're amazing."

"Overpower whoever comes." She nodded at his body. "You can kick some serious ass. Get off this shuttle and save yourself. I appreciate your honor but don't be stupid. You're worth a lot of money to the assholes running this ship. They could sell you on the black market to earn a fortune. I never would have turned you over to them if I hadn't believed you'd be returned to your people. I know a little something about being under someone's control. It sucks dirt. Now go, damn it. I'll find another chance to escape just as soon as I catch my breath and regain my strength."

He crossed two thickly muscled arms over his chest and Charlie realized for the first time that he'd changed his clothes. She'd been too busy in the attempt to save his ass while fighting to stay on her exhausted legs to really take a good look at him. The tank top revealed broad, dusky shoulders, two very muscular arms, and the pants he wore were black, snug breeches. His damp hair told her he'd used the room's cleansing unit to bathe.

"Your assumption of the crew is incorrect. They are returning me to a cyborg ship in less than twenty-four hours."

"Oh." *Damn. I could have gotten away.* "I just assumed we'd both been screwed."

"I appreciate you giving up your freedom."

A buzz sounded and Zorus crossed the room quickly, before the door opened. Charlie winced, waiting for whoever stood on the other side to enter the room to retrieve her. She hoped Gerald had ordered the men on the ship not to beat her down. While drugged, she knew she wouldn't be able to defend herself.

"You never said a word about tampering with my computer." Captain Varel's angry voice shouted. "I'd suspected you cyborgs were talented at that shit but I don't appreciate it. Return control to me now. I was notified of the change of command the way it's programmed to do the second you breached it."

Zorus' big body blocked the door. "I didn't do it. The female is well-versed in reprogramming, obviously. She's here with me and I'll have her return your systems to normal."

"Move," the captain ordered. "I'll teach her not to hack my ship."

Two big silvery-gray hands gripped the open doorway. "No. You won't harm the female for what she's done. Consider it a tradeoff for the pod she won't be using during her escape from the shuttle. I will need food for two sent immediately. Her body is in a much weakened condition."

"I don't give a damn," the captain huffed. "She took over my computer."

"No damage has been done." Zorus took on a bored tone. "She will reinstate order the second you leave to fetch food."

"Son of a bitch," the other man swore. "Fine. Don't allow her to do it again or I'll go through you to teach her that no one fucks with my ship."

"She will need clean clothing as well."

"What do I look like? Your employee?"

Zorus hesitated. "You are until your job is over." He backed up and the doors slid closed. He turned to stare at Charlie, meeting her confused gaze. "I'll fix what you did. Rest."

Charlie gaped at him. "But—"

"I have it." Zorus closed his eyes and seconds passed. He frowned but then slowly smiled. "Very intelligent. You short-circuited the identity scanner, pulled up the stored imprinted identifications, and recoded it to deceive the computer into believing you were Varel." Dark eyes snapped open. "I reset the system to ten minutes before you broke into the program to delete the changes you made. They will have to repair the physical damage to the panel you accessed but that is their problem."

"You can do that?" Charlie pushed up on wobbly arms. "How? You didn't even go near the access panel."

"I have remote abilities."

She bit her lip and then stared at him suspiciously. "Then why did I have to break you out of the medical facility? If you can hack at will, you easily could have freed yourself."

"They created me and were aware of my abilities. They kept me heavily drugged until they secured me inside a room with signal jammers. If you'll remember, they also kept me contained with chains. They weren't willing to risk electronic locks in case I was able to transmit shortwave signals strong enough to bypass the jamming."

"You should have told me that. If you had, I would have just escaped knowing you could take care of yourself if you wanted off this shuttle."

He shrugged. "You didn't tell me you could hack their systems either. We have that in common now as well."

Charlie gaped at him, astonished. "What is it with you and mentioning that?"

"I just find it fascinating that we share similar traits."

She took a deep breath and tried to ignore how her muscles quivered just from the struggle to hold her back above the mattress. She hated how weak she remained from the drugs. "Yeah," she said sarcastically. "It's like we're twins."

Zorus shook his head and folded his arms over his chest. "Your attempt at humor is definitely not a characteristic we share."

"That's true. I have a sense of humor and you don't."

Chapter Four

"True." Zorus admitted.

He couldn't stop studying the small human female reclined on his bed. Logic dictated that Charlie should have fled the shuttle when given the opportunity but instead she'd wasted her chance to escape with an attempt to rescue him as well. It greatly surprised him that a female would do that but the fact that she was human left him deeply disturbed.

His gaze landed on her shoulder where her shirt had been torn open by the human male on the docks. Dried blood caked her pale skin. He moved toward the cleansing unit. In a few steps he retrieved a small mobile unit and returned to the bed.

"I'm going to clean you."

Charlie watched him silently until she sank back onto the bed flat when her arms gave out. "Why aren't those guys dragging me out of here?"

"You're still a captive on their ship. I doubt it matters to them which room you remain inside as long as they know where you are."

That seemed to set her mind at ease when she nodded. "They sure can't take me back to the holding room they had me secured in. They know I could just get out again."

"True," he lied, not stating they could just drug her again. He eased down onto his knees next to the bed and hesitated. "Remove your shirt."

Uncertainty crossed her delicate features. "Why?"

"You're human and prone to infection. I wish to clean your injuries."

She still hesitated but then struggled to do as he'd instructed. Her body still fought the effects of the drug, which slowed her down, and sweat beaded her brow before she managed to wiggle enough to ease the shirt off. The black bra appeared stark compared to her very pale, creamy, white skin. Zorus tried to conceal his interest in the generous, soft mounds of flesh barely contained inside the thin material. He'd never seen a female with such large breasts before.

"What?"

He realized he'd failed to hide where his gaze kept straying when her hands lifted to cup her breasts in a sad attempt to shield them from his view. He watched with fascination until her cheeks bloomed pink from a blush. He leaned closer, intrigued by her show of modesty.

"I don't understand your question." He dropped the kit onto the bed, opened it, and removed a small can of foam spray. He lifted a cloth hand towel.

"You were staring at my boobs."

"I haven't seen them that size before." He didn't care how she took that statement.

"I thought you said you used to have to sleep with women." She frowned. "You lied?"

"No. I never slept with a human. I was forced to have sexual contact with them." He paused to control the anger those memories caused him to feel. "The humans never removed their shirts during those sessions." His focus drifted to the soft mounds cupped within her small hands, barely hiding any of the soft-looking flesh, still fascinated by the sight. "Cyborg females are more muscular and contain less fatty tissues."

"Nice description to use." She rolled her eyes. "I don't even want to hear what you have to say about my tummy. If your women are built the way you are, it's all muscle there, right?"

He lowered his attention to her waist and realized his hand moved of its own accord, his palm settling on top of her bare stomach between her bellybutton and the waist of her pants. His fingers gently dug into the soft skin there to discover the kind of pliability he'd never touched before. He enjoyed the sensation.

"Hey," her fingers curled around his wrist, a feeble attempt to dislodge his hold. "That tickles." She laughed.

Zorus jerked his head up to gape at her. She grinned at him. The transformation of her features did something strange to him. An unfamiliar emotion struck him and he pulled his hand away from her quickly. He did glance at her uncovered bra, which she'd had to release to grab his wrist. He savored the sight.

"I apologize. That wasn't my intention."

"I know I could lose a few pounds."

He refused to admit to her that she looked attractive to him. That paralyzed him for long seconds while he evaluated the sentiment. He dragged air into his lungs, noticed her feminine scent for the first time, and found it oddly pleasant. Worse, his body responded when his cock stiffened.

"This can't be happening."

"What?" Her smile faded and she peered up at him with curiosity.

"Nothing." He ignored his physical response and leaned over her to draw in more of her scent. He identified a mixture of vanilla and peaches that mingled with her natural chemistry. "Just relax while I wash away the blood."

"Okay. Thanks." She gave him another hesitant smile. "I appreciate it."

It's highly unlikely she'd appreciate it if I strip her naked to see if her thighs are as softly textured as her stomach. That thought made him close his eyes for a few heartbeats while he endured his cock hardening even more, until it dug into the unforgiving seam of the front closure of his pants. Anger instantly surfaced when he opened his eyes.

"Don't do that."

"Do what?"

"Smile at me."

Charlie's mouth parted but the smile faded. "Are you okay? Your face looks a little darker gray than normal."

"It's anger."

"What did I do to piss you off? Try to make light of the situation of me being half naked? I'm trying real hard not to feel uncomfortable and if you were a regular guy I'd be a little afraid."

"Regular guy? Explain that context to me."

"You know. A human guy. I know you're not interested in me as a woman, especially since you've made it no secret that you detest us. If I thought you had a sex drive geared toward women such as myself, well, this would be a real sticky situation."

He made sure to keep his lower body concealed to be certain she didn't notice the state of his very stimulated erection. "I understand."

Zorus took extra care to be gentle when he cleaned her shoulder to remove the dried blood and examined the scratches for signs of infection. Anger surfaced again at the sight of the angry marks marring her delicate skin. He regretted killing the dock worker so quickly. Now his preference would have been to make him suffer first.

"How bad is it? It stings a little."

"It's minimal. You'll heal within a week. I do not see any sign of infection but I'm going to obtain a med kit to be certain. Are you allergic to antibiotics?"

"No. At least I don't think so."

That drew alarm from him as he inched closer until his face hovered over hers. "You aren't certain what medications you may have adverse effects to?"

"I've never had them. I'm a grunt, remember? The government doesn't give out medicine to us. I may have worked in the better part of the city but it didn't raise my status any. They only allow us to move so we're able to get to work easier. They also hate to replace us and since murder rates are high in the slums, they put up with us living on the outer edge of the safe zones."

The list of diseases and infections that could have taken her life scrolled through his thoughts. It angered him. She wasn't a big female or overly robust. She actually looked a little frail to him and her softer, rounded body meant she didn't have a healthy exercise routine to gain an increased physical durability.

"What will you do when you reach Saturn?"

"Find my brother, make him give me half the money, and I'll start over. I sure can't return to Earth. By now they've figured out who helped you escape and they'll have issued an alert on me."

"Won't they send someone after you if you're living on Saturn?"

"Maybe, but they don't scan people as much there. If I live under the radar I can survive."

He quickly calculated her odds of avoiding detection. "Why not travel farther from Earth? Your odds are better."

"I'm a woman alone."

"I don't understand."

"You don't know much about what's going on, do you? Probably not," she answered her own question quickly. "Slave traders grab unprotected women and sell them to space whorehouses. That's if I'm lucky."

"You'd enjoy that lifestyle?" Everything he'd learned about her made him highly doubt that.

"Hell no." She glared at him. "Learn sarcasm. It's just the alternative is ending up captured by space pirates." Fear etched her features. "Do you know what those are?"

"Yes. We've come across those mutated humans who live in deep space. They carry diseases, are prone to extreme insanity, and usually attempt to breed any captured females. Our reports state that they don't have a high success rate. The females usually die pretty quickly."

"Exactly. I've also heard they turn cannibal sometimes and that's not my idea of a fun feast, considering I'm plump. I'm pretty certain I'd be on the wrong side of the table when it came time to pass out forks." Her gaze shifted to his chest. "Are you done? I'd like to put my shirt back on."

He had no logical reason to stop her but he shook his head anyway. "I ordered the captain to bring you a change of clothing. Yours are damaged."

"Do you want to back off then? If you get any closer, you're going to be on top of me."

An image flashed through his mind of doing exactly that and his cock twitched and his balls tightened until he suffered a dull ache. He softly cursed at such a strong reaction.

"What's wrong?"

The innocent expression on her face attracted him even more. For some reason she trusted him. It didn't make sense. As a female, she should be aware that no male could be honorable with half of her clothing removed.

"Are you stuck? Did your knees go to sleep? The floor is pretty unforgiving. I slammed mine into it when I collapsed in the hallway and it really hurt. If you hadn't picked me up I doubt I could have stood on my own immediately."

He backed up a little while his gaze traveled to her pants. "Let me check you for damage."

Her hands reached for her waist but instead of unfastening her pants, she gripped them tightly. "That's okay. I'm sure they're fine."

"Untreated wounds can cause infection." He dropped the cloth and easily pushed her hands out of the way. "Relax and don't fight me."

"I really don't think I'm hurt." She tried to swat his hands away but he ignored her feeble attempt, her weakened condition still present.

Zorus jerked her pants open and tugged them down. She couldn't put up much of a fight with her sluggish responses. He easily slid them down to her ankles and jerked off her boots to totally remove the pants. He also removed her socks. His gaze lingered on the small scrap of red panties hiding her sex.

"That's not my knees." Her hands cupped between her thighs, covering the silky material. "Do you need to upgrade a program covering human anatomy?"

"There's nothing wrong with my memory. Cyborg and human anatomy is the same." He tried not to ogle her breasts as they strained the black, skimpy material but the incredibly tempting curve of her creamy flesh pressing outward from the tight, small article of clothing, called to him. He barely remembered that he needed to examine her knees, but as his attention lowered down her stomach to her pale thighs, her knees were the last thing he wanted to study. "I'm going to scan you for injury."

He placed his palms at the top of her thighs. They were as soft and supple as they appeared, perhaps even more so, and he traced them down to her knees. A slight redness marked them.

"You may have some bruising. Bend them up."

Charlie tried to remember to breathe. The cyborg's hands were warm and gentle, more of a caress than a touch. If he were human she'd swear he did it on purpose but he'd been real clear that he held no interest in her as a woman.

"What do you want me to do?"

He frowned at her and his brown eyes seemed darker than normal. "Bend your knees up. Tell me if it hurts."

She ordered her racing heart to slow. He just wanted to make sure she hadn't broken anything. *It's no big deal. He's acting similar to a medic, probably training he has been given, and I'm the only one taking this as anything sexual.* She repeated that twice inside her head before she followed his instructions to draw her legs upward and pulled her heels closer to her ass.

"No pain but I think you're right."

"About what?" His attention seemed riveted on her thighs again.

"The bruising. They feel a little tender."

He made a soft noise.

"What was that?"

He lifted his gaze to her and his expression seemed really tense. "Are you curious?"

"About what? If I'm bruised?"

He distinctively growled and anger flashed across his handsome features. "No. I'm curious, and while I'm trying to ignore it, I no longer wish to."

"What are you talking about?"

His hands had released her when she'd repositioned her legs but he gripped her gently again, this time to wrap them around the curve of her knees. To her shock, he spread her thighs, parted her feet too, until it left her wide open on the cot. He bent over her until his torso pinned one leg flat to the mattress before he released that leg. One hand slid hers away from covering her panties.

Charlie's eyes widened as the heat from his palm registered when he cupped her sex. He had a big hand that covered not only her pussy but part of her lower stomach. Her gaze jerked to his to find him watching her with a definite frown.

"I won't hurt you."

She lay paralyzed with astonishment, not even breathing. When she sucked in air to her starved lungs, she gasped loudly. "What are you doing?"

"What do you think?" His palm slowly slid upward and then back to rub against her clit. "Are you attached to this garment?"

Her brain froze, leaving her unable to think while he rubbed her again but this time the pad of his thumb slipped through the side of the thin material to locate the small bud of nerves to massage it in tight, firm circles. Shock transformed into pleasure.

"Answer me," his gruff voice demanded.

She couldn't look away from his dark gaze but she found her voice again and the ability to move. She tried to move the leg he gripped but his hold kept her still. The drugs had worked somewhat out of her system but walking from her quarters to his had left her pretty weak.

"What are you doing?" She breathed the question softly.

"You saved my life and you said I should get on my knees to show my gratitude. I've considered it and decided it's a good way to repay you."

His thumb released her clit to grip the middle of her panties. Material tore with the help of a firm tug. The sound registered to Charlie at the same time air hit her now exposed pussy. She jerked but before she could react in any other way, he tossed aside the damaged panties, and turned his head back to lower it.

Her entire body tensed when his fingers spread her open and a really hot, wet, strong tongue teased her clit. Charlie gasped in more air and threw her head back. She frantically grabbed for anything just to clutch at something. Her fingers dug into her bent thigh he had pinned and she ended up with a handful of his silky hair.

Zorus had no mercy while he flicked his tongue against her clit quickly, causing raw, nearly painful ecstasy to spread lightning quick from it straight to her brain. Her eyes closed and her hips arched closer to his talented mouth. Moans tore from her throat.

The climax slammed her hard and fast, bowing her body, and shook her to the core of her soul. He didn't ease up either, just continued to torment her until she jerked violently. She heard someone begging and realized the ragged voice belonged to her.

Zorus tore his mouth away and Charlie's entire body went limp. The mattress dipped and she realized her eyes were closed so she opened them in time to watch Zorus crawl up her body. One of his hands planted near her head to hold up his weight while he reached between them.

She couldn't speak, wasn't sure what to say, and her body still twitched from how hard she'd come. She knew she should feel embarrassed at how fast he'd gotten her off but the cyborg knew exactly how to tongue her in a way to set off an explosive fireworks display inside her body.

His gaze fused with hers when he slowly lowered his body on top of her. His weight pressed her down against the soft mattress but not enough to crush. It dawned on her what was about to happen but she didn't tell him to stop. She wasn't sure if she really wanted him but her nearly sated body ached for more. She got it when the thick-tipped, hard crown of his cock nudged against her soaked labia, parted them, and slowly pressed against the opening of her pussy. Her hands rose to clutch at his shoulders when he pressed inside her.

Charlie wrapped her legs around the back of his thighs, accepting him when he eased deeper into her channel. Pleasure drew throaty moans from her again and her hips tilted to accept him more easily. Zorus groaned softly and his passion-filled eyes narrowed as she stared up at him in wonder.

She knew with conviction, in that moment, that no one had ever made her feel this good before and she had once been certain that Gerald would always remain the best lover she'd ever had. She'd been wrong, she admitted silently, when Zorus pulled back, nearly withdrew totally from her

74

body, and then smoothly entered her again, going deeper and stretching awake wonderful nerve endings that sent rapture straight into her brain.

"Amazing," he groaned, slowly thrusting in and out of her.

She agreed. Her knees bent more, her legs wrapped higher around him until her calves locked over his round, firm ass. He sank into her deeper and lowered even more until their bodies rubbed against each other in a delicious teasing manner that had her panting and clawing at his shoulders where her nails bit into skin. Her hips bucked under him to urge him on.

"Faster...please," she pleaded.

Zorus groaned and nuzzled her face aside. His mouth brushed her throat when she turned her face away to give him what he wanted. Teeth raked the top of her shoulder, notched up her desire, and then his strong hips hammered her fast and hard.

"Oh god," she panted. "Yes!"

The pleasure built into a frenzy of driving need and then Charlie screamed out as she came again, harder this time than the last, and Zorus threw his head back to shout when he found his own release. Charlie's eyes flew open as hot heat flooded her inside. She could actually feel his thick shaft pulse against her quivering vaginal walls when he came.

He collapsed, his face resting next to hers, but kept enough weight braced with his elbows for her to still be able to draw air into her lungs. The sound of their ragged breathing mingled and his hot breath tickled the side of her throat, damp from his kisses and love bites. Charlie wrapped her arms around his neck and secured her legs tightly around his waist to hold him against her in case he tried to withdraw from her body. She didn't want to break their connection. *At least not yet.*

"Are you well?" The cyborg's voice came out a little gruff.

"Yes."

"You're so small and fragile. I must be smothering you."

"I'm good." She hesitated a second and then opened her mouth. She brushed a kiss on his throat, used a little tongue to taste him, but stopped when he tensed suddenly. "What? I can't kiss you?"

Zorus lifted his head and his dark gaze studied her. "You want to kiss me?"

The stunned look on his features made her smile. "Don't cyborgs do that?"

"No. At least not in my experience."

"Don't you have sex? I mean, you're really good at it."

"I have sex regularly."

That bit of information left an unhappy ball of misery inside her gut. She didn't like the idea of him with someone else though she knew she had no right to feel jealous. He wasn't hers, they weren't in a relationship, but the green monster remained.

"Oh."

"I don't kiss my sexual partners."

"You kissed my neck."

"I stimulated an erogenous zone to bring you to orgasm since I couldn't reach the others in this position."

76

"It felt like a kiss to me."

He arched one eyebrow. "I'm not opposed if you want to kiss me."

She pulled her arms down and cupped his handsome face. "When is the last time you actually kissed someone on the mouth?"

A slow frown curved his generous mouth. "Never."

Flabbergasted, Charlie couldn't form words.

"I refused to allow humans to kiss me during sex acts and the female cyborgs have never asked me to do that when we arrange meetings."

"Meetings?" She got that out, too astonished at his claim to never have been kissed to really say much more.

"I'm not a member of a family unit. I'm sterile and as a high ranking council member I'm not required to join one since it would be pointless. I can't donate to the gene pool of my race and the only benefit of contracting with a female would be access to her body. If I have a need for physical contact with one, there are plenty of them willing to exchange sexual intercourse for favors my position allows me to give."

Charlie tried to make sense of his words. "You can't have kids? Is that what you mean?"

"Affirmative. Since I was used for sex after I'd been created they made it impossible for my body to impregnate any female after discovering I had that capability. There is no reversing what has been done to me."

"And you only have sex with cyborg women who want you to do them political favors?"

He frowned. "You are abnormally pale."

"It sounds so cold," she whispered, sadness filling her. "And they don't even kiss you?"

"There is no reason. It's about mutual sexual gratification without emotion attachment."

Her hands caressed his jawline and cheeks. "Do you know how to kiss?"

He hesitated. "I believe so."

"Close your eyes."

"Why?"

"I'm going to kiss you. Relax and just feel."

Charlie lifted her head and closed her own eyes, not sure if he did, and her mouth gently brushed against his. His lips were surprisingly pliable, soft, and he allowed her to part them when she used her tongue to tease the bottom one. She entered his mouth, totally in control of the kiss, and on unsure ground since she'd never kissed someone who had never done it before.

Inside her his cock stirred, fluttered, and noticeably hardened. It urged her to get more aggressive. She swept his mouth, rasping her tongue over his, and she turned her head a little to get more access. He started to kiss her back, their tongues dancing together, merging and stroking.

Zorus groaned and started to move his hips, fucking her leisurely to match his movements with their kiss. Charlie moaned and her hands slid down his throat, his chest, and moved around his waist, to rake her nails down his spine. He drove into her hard and deep, breaking the seal of their lips when they both cried out in pleasure.

It was Zorus who took possession of her mouth as soon as he started to glide into her again and picked up the pace of their rocking joined bodies. Charlie clung to him, kissing him with a desperation that drove their passion higher until she tore away from him to avoid biting his tongue when another climax tore through her. He cried out seconds later and came deep inside her.

Chapter Five

Zorus woke first, surprised he'd fallen asleep. He'd obviously rolled them over on the narrow bed at some point during the sleep cycle since Charlie's body draped his with him under her. Her weight resting over his chest and hips didn't unsettle him as much as the instant memories of what they'd done together.

He lifted his hand from the small of her back and touched his lips, reliving the kisses they'd shared. They felt a little swollen to him but in a way that made him want to smile. He flexed his other hand only to realize he held soft flesh in his palm. He eased his hold on her ass. Charlie mumbled something against his chest. Her head rested there, sideways, her ear pressed over his heart. Her long hair ran across his ribs, trapped between them and his arm.

Sex had never been more explosive as it had been with the woman who slept atop his body. It held no logic for him but he couldn't deny the truth. Charlie, a human, had made him feel more in one night than he'd ever felt in his entire existence. An unfamiliar emotion surfaced and he didn't try to suppress it. Instead he evaluated what it could be. It startled him when the answer came and his body tensed while every muscle tightened in protest.

His arm wrapped protectively around Charlie's back to cradle her against him and he didn't want to let her go. Possession and an undeniable urge to keep her made him wrap his other arm around her to hold on tighter. Determination grew with every breath he took while he ordered his body to relax.

The odds of her being willing to stay with him were not in his favor. She wished to get revenge on her deceitful brother who'd betrayed her trust. The human, Russell, wasn't of consequence but convincing her not to follow him to Saturn would be difficult. He could just take her and force her to remain at his side until his fascination waned but that would defeat the purpose of figuring out why she affected him so deeply and strangely.

Her breathing changed and her head lifted. Zorus met her sleepy gaze and she did something odd. She smiled at him. Her dark hair had become a tangled mess while she slept or perhaps it could have happened from the sexual encounters they had shared. She still had the power to make him want her even though she didn't look her best. That curve upward of her mouth had his cock reacting, stiffening as blood rushed to his groin.

"Morning."

He reached out with his mind to connect to the onboard computer. "It's actually afternoon. We slept for ten hours."

She laughed and flattened her hands on top of his chest, using the back of them to rest her chin on while she studied his face. "We had a tough evening. It's no wonder we were out for so long."

"Did I hurt you?"

"No. I admit I'm feeling some aching muscles I didn't realize I had but I'm just hungry mostly."

Anger surged. "I ordered the captain to bring food and clothing for you. He never did."

"I think I heard the door ding but we were busy." She winked. "You're not a happy person in the mornings, are you?"

"I'm not unhappy."

"Just grumpy then." Her focus lowered to his chest. "I bet I could put a smile on your face." She wiggled her hips a little, indicating that she wanted him to release her waist.

Zorus hesitated and then unwound his arms to place them flat at his sides. He didn't want to let her go but it just wasn't logical to force her to remain sprawled over his body. Instead of climbing off, she slipped down his body and her knees slid from the sides of his hips to the inside of his thighs. He spread them to make room until she sat back on her calves. He looked down with interest to see what she'd do.

"You can't change my emotions."

"Wow," she ignored his comment. "You're impressive, Zorus."

He drew his arms up and crossed them behind his head to improve his view of her. Charlie seemed mesmerized with his erect cock. Her hand rose to wrap around the base of his shaft. He tensed instantly.

"What are you doing?"

"Exploring you." She bit her lower lip and then released it with her teeth to slide her tongue across both. She glanced up with a smile again. "You're big all over. I can turn your grumpy attitude into a better one."

"That's just not—"

She moved quickly and his arms shot out to grab at her but when her mouth closed over the tip of his cock his hands froze inches from making contact to knock her away. He'd thought for an instant that she might be attacking. Her mouth was warm and wet as it encased the tip of his throbbing sex. The sensation of her tongue making circles to trace the edge of the crown made him groan.

She sucked on him, taking more, and he locked his hips in place so he wouldn't rock against her mouth and force his cock in too deep. All thoughts left him while he just enjoyed the pleasure she created when she started to slowly lift and lower her head and turn her face to different angles. He didn't try to block the gratification or get control of it. Instead he watched her, grew more aroused, and warned her before he came.

He expected her to release him but instead she moved faster, quickening the delicious friction of the wet, tight seal that her heated, wonderful mouth created. Zorus threw his head back, his balls tightening until it nearly hurt, and then he started to jerk under her while his semen emptied into her welcoming throat. She swallowed him down, making him cry out more with each suckle, until he couldn't stand it anymore. It had become too intense. His fingers tangled with her hair to tug her off him, trying not to harm her.

Charlie released him and he heard her chuckle before she climbed up his body. His hold on her hair eased, withdrew, and she collapsed on top of his chest once more, careful to keep his still-hard cock from becoming trapped between their bodies when she straddled his lower stomach. He could feel how wet she'd become as her sex rubbed against his skin.

He slowly opened his eyes to find her face hovering over his and a grin lighting up her attractive features. She licked her lips before she spoke. "Let's try this again. Good morning."

He rolled them over, careful not to crush her leg at the side of his hip, and pinned her under him. Her eyes widened with surprise a second before he drove into her welcoming pussy. She threw her head back, her fingers clawed at his biceps, and pure possessiveness gripped him when he buried himself into her as deeply as he could get. He froze there, held still, enjoying how hot and tight and wet she was for him.

Charlie wrapped her legs around his hips, her heels dug into his ass, and she met his gaze. "You just came. How can you—"

"I'm not a human male," he informed her. "I can fuck you for hours."

"You're going to kill me if you do." She grinned to soften the severity of her words. "But I'd sure appreciate it if you'd move long enough to make me feel really good."

He slowly pulled back, almost completely left the wonderful soft sheath of her pussy and then drove home, deep, making her cry out in pleasure. Her legs squeezed him tightly to hold him against her and he braced his knees into the soft bed, spread her thighs wider when he lifted up a little until it forced her ass to lift off the mattress. He started to pound into her steadily and quickly while he adjusted the angle of his cock with the sounds she made, telling him what caused her the most pleasure.

The muscles of her vaginal walls tightened even more until he almost fought to get into and out of her, watched her features tense, her eyes widen, and then her mouth parted when she cried out his name. He snarled, satisfied that she knew without a doubt who had made her climax, and unclenched his teeth. He had been fighting his own release to make sure she reached hers first. He threw his head back, drove into her even faster, and her convulsing sex squeezed and milked him into sexual oblivion. Rapture blinded him, detonated inside his brain and body, and he knew nothing for long seconds until the haze of it passed.

"Can't breathe," Charlie gasped softly, her hands pushing at his shoulders.

He jerked his weight up enough to stop crushing her. "I'm sorry." It horrified him that he'd totally lost all control over his body and that he'd collapsed completely on top of her in a wilted mass.

She gasped in air and then surprised him again when she laughed. "I'm okay. I'm actually pretty great." Her hands cupped his face. "You don't need to shave, do you?"

He shook his head, more than a little confused. "I can't follow your logic."

"My logic?"

"We had intercourse, I nearly suffocated you, and out of the blue, you ask about facial hair?"

She laughed. "It was great sex, I take it as a compliment that you nearly fell comatose after fucking me, and I just noticed you have no stubble on your face. What's not to understand about that?"

Charlie tried not to laugh but she couldn't help it. He was so cute with that baffled look on his face. Yesterday she'd been sure he won the award for biggest asshole she'd ever met but a night with him, sharing his bed, had shown her a whole new side of Zorus. A sexy, incredibly hot one that had sent her libido into overdrive and left her body singing his praises, if not also a bit sore from all the physical activity.

She'd never slept with a man she hadn't been totally involved with in a long-term relationship but she didn't suffer any regrets. The feel of him still connected to her by their joined bodies gave her an odd sensation of rightness that should have unsettled her but it didn't, for some reason. They were both in over their heads. Obviously neither of them had foreseen that they'd end up in bed together, and that made her feel even more connected to him on an emotional level.

"Are you making fun of me?"

"No." She couldn't wipe off the smile. "I'm not but I find this kind of amusing."

"I don't."

She studied his features and saw anger begin to darken his beautiful eyes. "What we just shared was smoking hot and you just called it intercourse. That sounds so cold. Don't you see the irony in that?"

He blinked a few times. "No."

She saw the truth in his sincere gaze. "You confuse me too," she admitted. "You can be computerlike but when we touch, you're the exact opposite."

"I don't understand."

"Right now you're reminding me of one of the computers I have interaction with. When you're touching me though..." She decided to be blunter. "When you're having sex with me, you are really passionate and alive. Do you understand?"

"That I understand. We connect better during intercourse than on a conversational level."

"Can you stop calling it that?"

"Intercourse?"

"Yeah. It sounds so clinical and what we did together was anything but."

"Do you prefer the term fucking?" He actually arched an eyebrow and his eyes shone with amusement.

"I like that word better."

"I assumed that word would insult your feminine sensibilities."

"Another thing they programmed you with?"

Zorus took a deep breath. "I'm not a computer, nor do I have chips that function as my brain. I have chips and implants installed into my organic brain that help me control certain physical functions but I'm completely sentient."

"You talk the way computers do sometimes." She didn't want to insult him. "I'm glad I'm not doing an android though."

"I'm a cyborg." Anger tensed his muscles.

"I'm not real sure what that means or what the differences are. I don't mean to piss you off or insult you. Whatever you are, I obviously like you a hell of a lot." She wiggled her hips, noticed his cock had softened somewhat inside her, and stopped moving to prevent dislodging him. She wanted to stay the way they were and feared he'd emotionally withdraw from her if he did physically. "Talk to me."

"I'm a laboratory-engineered super being with spliced genes and cloning technology. I have chips implanted in sections of my brain that enable me to shut off the signals a normal brain sends." He paused. "I have some artificial organs and cybernetic technology to replace damaged or defective parts of my body."

Charlie tried not to show how his words affected her. *What the hell had they done to Zorus and the people created like him?* It sounded awful and horrifying. She caressed his cheek.

"So you are part human and part robotics?"

He hesitated. "We don't consider ourselves human even though we were created from human DNA. Our DNA was mutated, enhanced, spliced into what the scientists wished us to be and then we were grown with cloning technology in vats. I detest being compared to an android. Our bodies are mostly made up of organic materials with cybernetic enhancements." He lowered his face until their noses touched. "Do you understand the difference?"

"Yes. You're definitely not a computer or an android." His body relaxed again on hers, making her aware of how much he'd tensed up without her noticing.

"Exactly."

"Then why do you talk the way they do?"

"Why does your race and others solely depend on technology to enhance your lives?"

"Computers are smarter than people."

He suddenly smiled. "My race aspires to be better than humanity."

She stared into his eyes and nodded. "I think I get it but it's not so bad being more emotional."

"I wouldn't know." He grew serious. "I rarely allow myself to experience emotion."

"You should. I like you better when you stop thinking and just let your body take over."

Something flashed across his face but then it was gone before she could guess at what he'd felt.

"Why?"

"You can be one cold asshole when you want to be. I didn't like you much at all before last night."

"Yet you still gave up your chance to escape this shuttle by attempting to rescue me. Explain to me why you did that. I can't make sense of it. It's just not logical why you'd do that for me."

Her sense of humor kicked in. "I guess I have a soft spot for assholes."

He withdrew from her body, lowered his a few inches, but kept her pinned under him. "I want the real reason."

"I'm not sure but I kind of liked you for some odd reason. Not to mention that you did save me from being raped. You didn't have to do that. It gave me hope that you had redeeming qualities and I was justified in believing that."

Zorus studied her features. "We have things in common."

"There's that too. Of course we have a lot of things that are polar opposites."

"Opposites can attract."

His response surprised her and she smiled. "I've heard that before but never believed it until now."

He suddenly glanced at the door. "The captain is coming."

"How do you know?"

Zorus flattened his palms on the bed and pushed up then climbed off the bed and bent to pull on his pants. "I've been connected to the onboard computer since we woke. We're less than an hour from docking with a ship hired by my people to pick me up and take me home." He turned his head, his dark gaze fixing on her. "Put on my shirt."

She accepted the one he'd worn the night before, slid it over her head and got to her feet as the door dinged. Zorus closed his pants and moved barefoot to the door. He braced his hands on the frame, using his body to block it when the door slid open.

"I brought you the clothes for the woman and the food. I tried to deliver them before but you didn't answer." Captain Varel attempted to step into the room.

Zorus didn't budge. "Thank you. You may just hand them over. There's no reason for you to enter my room." He released the frame to put out his hands.

"Fine. Here. We dock with a shuttle in sixty-eight minutes. Be ready to leave the ship."

"We will be."

Charlie didn't miss the "we". Her heart had speeded up inside her chest as she waited for the captain to protest but he hadn't. He'd just handed Zorus a bundle of folded clothing and a tray of food. Zorus backed up and the door slid firmly closed. He turned, his expression grim.

"We'll eat, use the cleansing unit, and prepare to transfer."

"They are going to allow me to go with you?" She didn't believe that. "What about Gerald?"

"I convinced the captain not to deliver you to the man who purchased you."

"How?" Uneasiness rose inside her. "What did you do? When did you do it?"

He ignored her questions when he crossed the room to sit on the bed next to her. He dropped the clothing on the end of it and turned a little to place the tray across his thighs. "Who is the human who attempted to buy you from your brother?"

She met his dark gaze and saw anger there. "When I was younger I used to date him. We were lovers."

Definitely anger. The cyborg's fist clenched the metal tray hard enough to dent it. The sound of metal bending made him stop. "You had intercourse with this male?"

"We were together for a few years. I thought we'd marry and have kids. I believed I loved him but then this rich woman took an interest in him. He had a job dealing with the upper-class, training them in self defense. She wanted to marry him and he dumped me to go live in her world."

91

Oh yeah. Fury darkened his eyes and the metal dented enough at the corner where he gripped it until the entire thing curved downward. She reached out and tugged, trying to take it from him before their breakfast hit the floor. He released it to her and both of his hands fisted over his thighs while he glowered.

"It was a long time ago," she explained, stunned that he'd be jealous. She was certain that had to be why he looked mad enough to hit something. "Gerald started sniffing around me again a few months after his marriage, wanting me to agree to be his mistress."

"That's a female sexual partner a male obtains besides possessing a primary sexual partner, correct?"

"Yes." She set the tray on her lap, looking away from Zorus. "The bastard thought I'd jump at the chance to be with him after he ripped my heart out." She shook her head and sighed. "As if I could ever forgive him for walking out on me and breaking my heart. Do you see the word 'stupid' stamped across my forehead?"

Zorus glanced up. "No."

Charlie laughed. "Rhetorical question."

"You have no forgiveness for males who betray your trust and abandon you."

"No, I don't. Would you have forgiven that?"

The anger in his eyes left. "Do you still love him?"

"Hell no."

"Good." He dropped his gaze to the food and reached for one of the sandwiches piled on a plate. "I'm glad to hear that."

Charlie grinned but didn't say anything, stuffing food into her mouth instead. Zorus admitted to being glad—an emotion—and she wasn't even sure he'd realized it. They ate in silence until they finished everything on the tray and didn't speak until Zorus stood.

"I'll use the cleansing unit first." His dark gaze settled on her. "You won't attempt to leave, will you?"

"They are going to let me go with you, aren't they?"

"Yes."

"Then there's no reason to try to get off the shuttle without you."

"Good. I will hurry."

"At the first port, I need to obtain transportation to Saturn. Can you get your cyborg people to drop me off at one?"

His features tensed. "We'll discuss that at a later date."

"I want to discuss it now. Am I going to be safe with your people?"

"No one will harm you, Charlie. I give you my word on that. There's no reason for alarm."

"Then you're going to have them drop me off somewhere so I can find passage to Saturn?"

He shifted his stance and then stalked toward the corner. "Yes."

Charlie watched him disappear into the cleansing unit and heard it turn on a minute later. She sighed loudly while staring at the closed door that separated her from Zorus. She admitted that she'd miss him more than just a little when they said goodbye. She trusted his word that he'd make sure she got off the shuttle they were about to board and get safe passage to a port.

She had a brother to track down. Russell would pay for what he'd done to her. First she'd kick his ass and then make him give up half the money. After that he would be on his own since she'd never trust him again. She'd be all alone.

An image of Zorus flashed inside her head, his intense brown eyes. She pushed it back. It would be crazy to even consider trying to track him down after she took care of business. They were too different and he wouldn't welcome her if she showed up at a future date to take up where they were about to leave off.

"Me and my attraction to men all wrong for me," she muttered. "Stupid, Charlie. Don't even go there. He's a cyborg and he doesn't even like humans." Her gaze drifted to the messed-up bed she still sat on and she grimaced. "At least out of bed."

Chapter Six

Nervousness had Charlie tugging at the oversized shirt she wore for at least the twentieth time. She hated not having a weapon except for the knife hidden inside her boot while she stood next to Zorus. Nine men surrounded them inside the cargo bay of the shuttle. Captain Varel looked grim when they docked with another shuttle.

"You remain here." The captain nodded at his men. "I'll be back when they have paid and you can release them then." The doors opened to allow him to leave the shuttle with a few of the crew.

Zorus turned his head to peer down at her. "Enough fidgeting. There's no reason for it. This transfer will go smoothly. My people will pay and we'll board their shuttle."

"I'm not fidgeting." She gave him an innocent look while lying, refusing to admit her fear of what awaited her when they came in contact with more cyborgs or how out of place she felt. Time seemed to crawl by until she wondered what took so long.

Zorus clenched his teeth, a muscle jumped along his jawline, and he didn't seem to enjoy the wait either. One of the crew smiled suddenly and nodded. The money had been paid.

They both faced the doors when the sound of the airlock softly filled the room. The noise reminded Charlie of a deflating balloon. It slid open as the crew backed up. Captain Varel smiled when he returned to the shuttle.

Zorus gave him a slight incline of his head. "Thank you."

"No, thank you." Varel looked really pleased.

Charlie followed Zorus onto another shuttle through a narrow docking sleeve. The instant they entered the small cargo hold, fear gripped her as she gaped at five large cyborgs who wore all black leather from their necks to their booted feet. Even the hands of some of the men were covered with black leather gloves. One cyborg with jet-black hair that fell to his shoulders stepped forward. His blue eyes were cold and he appeared downright mean when he scowled at Zorus.

"Councilman Zorus." He gave a slight nod. "You look well."

Zorus reached back and gripped Charlie's upper arm to pull her none-too-gently against his side, and kept her there. "You should better hide your disappointment at my survival."

The mean-looking cyborg didn't deny it. "We have a cabin ready for you. We're giving you the captain's quarters."

Zorus hesitated. "Flint, are we currently free from danger from Earth Government?"

Flint inclined his head. "Yes." His gaze cut to Charlie. "And we're settled up over you buying the woman."

Charlie tensed, her mind trying to digest what she'd heard, but Zorus strode toward the other cyborg across the cargo hold, hauling her with him. She stumbled but he kept going. His strength all but pulled her through the room toward an interior shuttle door. She glanced around to take in her surroundings and spotted a human woman who stood next to a tall, fierce-looking, bald cyborg who mostly blocked the sight of her with his big body.

No one looked particularly happy. One of the cyborgs suddenly moved into their path. Zorus came to a halt.

"What did he mean about buying me?" Charlie ignored the other cyborg to peer up in surprise at Zorus. She jerked hard on his arm to get his attention.

Zorus gave no hint of his emotions. "I had to buy you from the humans to obtain your release."

She swallowed the lump that formed in her throat. He could have left her to Gerald's mercy or the crew of that shuttle but he'd paid them off instead to get her free. It touched her deeply that he'd care that much. It also made tears of gratitude prick her eyes. He really wasn't a bastard after all or an asshole.

"Why would you do that? How much money do I owe you?"

Zorus hesitated. He peered around the room more carefully instead of looking at her. "Which ship is this? I don't recognize it."

Charlie reached out to touch Zorus on his arm. "Talk to me. How much do I owe you?"

Flint answered Zorus. "It's not one of ours. We borrowed it from the human female over there. Her name is Jillian and she's involved with Coal." He jerked his head in the direction of the woman with the scary-looking bald cyborg. "We didn't want to bring one of our ships this close to Earth in case they identified them as stolen. The last thing we need would be a run-in with Earth Government. We're going to meet the *Star* and *Rally* when we're safely out of range. From there we'll take you home where the council awaits you. I'm supposed to send you their regards and well sentiments regarding your safe return."

Zorus nodded. "I want clothing and a secure com link to the council."

"Fine." Flint moved closer to study them both with a frown. "Who is she and what do you want done with her?"

"She belongs to me." Zorus stated coldly. "She isn't your concern."

A horrified expression transformed the tall cyborg's features and he definitely shot her a look filled with pity as his voice lowered. "I know you hate humans and are always looking for a way to torment them but please allow me to give her to one of the men instead."

A gray-haired cyborg who'd blocked them from leaving the cargo hold suddenly drew closer. Charlie couldn't help but gape at him. His hair appeared the same shade of gray as elderly people had but he looked no older than his early thirties. His eyes were a pale blue, nearly glowing with enough white in them to make her wonder if he were sightless, but then his gaze locked directly with hers.

"Give the human female to me, Councilman Zorus." He glared at him then. "I've taken enough of your shit for you to owe me. I'll even buy her from you."

Zorus tensed. "No, Sky."

Charlie released his arm when the tension between them radiated enough for her to sense a fight brewing. They were both big, powerfully built cyborgs. She wasn't sure what was going on but her inner alarms screamed warnings at her.

"Damn you," Sky hissed. "Did she do something to you while you were on Earth? Is that it? She's a female. I won't allow you to torture and kill her the way I've seen you do to a few of the male humans you've gotten your vicious hands on. You enjoyed beating them to death but I'll be damned if I watch you do that to a woman, human or not."

"Silence," Zorus demanded, his tone icy. "They deserved it."

"She doesn't." Sky advanced, going chest to chest with Zorus, his voice rising in volume. "You're a sick bastard who gets off on killing humans. You even made a few of them believe you were their friend before you attacked. You're the one who demanded all humans be made nothing but property on our planet and you've tried to order every female killed who hooked up with one of us. I'm sorry you survived, if you want the truth. I'd have been happier if you'd died on Earth. I won't stand by and watch you turn on this female. You've killed your last damn human." He pushed Zorus hard. "I want ownership of her and I'll fight you for it."

Charlie jumped out of the way when Zorus slammed hard into the bulkhead. Horror at what she'd heard left her grasping to make sense of it. Her gaze flew to Zorus when he pushed away from the wall, rage twisting his features. The other cyborg said he'd killed humans after befriending them. That horror sank in slowly and when Zorus glanced at her, he didn't deny any of it. Instead he looked away before he lunged to go after the other cyborg.

Their bodies hit hard, one of them grunted, and then they went down onto the cargo floor. The other cyborgs rushed forward to separate the two fighting men. They managed to pull them apart by dragging them away from each other but not before more punches were exchanged between Zorus and Sky.

Her brain jolted from the distress of knowing she had once again been lied to and betrayed by a man she trusted. Zorus wasn't even liked by his own people and he obviously had lulled her into believing him by using his sexual skills. Pain burned hot inside her chest and tears nearly blinded her at how easily he'd manipulated her into buying all the bullshit he'd said to her. He hated all humans and planned to kill her.

One of the cyborgs backed up closer to her, his arms wrapped around Zorus to pin his arms to his sides from behind, and Charlie saw the weapon strapped to his hip. She grabbed at it, surprised when she found it in her grip, and stumbled back. Her hand shook when she raised the weapon, not sure who to point it at. She put more space between her and everyone inside the cargo hold just as they realized what she'd done.

The cyborgs released their holds on Sky and Zorus, going for their own weapons. Terror threatened to give her a heart attack when she stared at five deadly cyborgs taking aim at her so fast she couldn't believe they were able to move that quickly.

"Drop the weapon," one of them demanded.

"Easy," Flint ordered softly but his own weapon pointed at her head. "Put it down, human. Otherwise we will kill you."

"Don't shoot," Zorus roared, spinning around to face her now that he wasn't restrained. He stepped directly in front of her and blocked her body from the weapons aimed at her. "If you kill her, I'll kill the one who fires." His gaze locked with hers. "Charlie, trust me."

She shook her head and her hand trembled harder. She realized with him standing where he'd moved that the only clear shot she had would kill him because her weapon pointed directly at the middle of his chest. She moved it to target his shoulder instead. She just couldn't kill him, regardless of how badly he'd hurt her with his lies. Winging him though, to get out of this mess, wouldn't cause her any sleepless nights. *At least not too many.*

Zorus took a slow step closer, his hands opening at his side. "I'd never harm you. You know that."

"I don't know what to think," she admitted, her voice shaking worse. "Please don't come any closer. I don't want to have to hurt you."

"Move out of the way," one of the cyborgs ordered Zorus. "We don't have a clear shot."

"Let her shoot him," Sky urged. "Just don't kill her. Aim for her shoulder so she'll survive. She's just terrified."

Zorus didn't budge, his intense brown eyes still locked on her. "Charlie, listen to me. Those humans I killed were bounty hunters sent after cyborgs. I had to befriend them to learn truthful information from them. They wanted to locate the planet we settled on to get a fix on it to give Earth Government the ability to send battle cruisers to take us out. I needed them to trust me to discover what information they'd learned so far to sell to Earth. They would have turned us in for the bounty on our heads without a second thought. Releasing them or allowing them to live wouldn't have been feasible. They would have escaped the first chance they were given and I had to protect my people."

Her hand wavered. She really wanted to believe him but she knew he could be a real asshole. "I trusted my brother and look where that got me. I just can't trust you. There's too much at stake if I'm wrong."

"She's smart," Sky muttered loud enough for her to hear.

Zorus turned his head to glare at the other cyborg. "Shut up. That's an order. I'm still a councilman and your superior."

Charlie glanced toward Sky and spotted him about ten feet away, to the left of Zorus. He looked pissed off but his lips pressed tightly together. From the corner of her eye, she saw movement and focused back on Zorus but he lunged at her. She didn't have time to react.

His body slammed into her shoulder when he tackled her, throwing her arm back to avoid the weapon, and she hit the floor hard. Pain exploded inside her head when it hit the unforgiving metal surface. Weight crushed her as she fought to stay conscious. The heavy body on top of hers shifted off her chest until she could breathe again. Zorus yanked the gun from her numb fingers and then peered down at her. He looked furious.

"Get a medic," he snarled. "Her head is bleeding."

Charlie passed out.

* * * * *

Zorus paced the room, boiling with rage, and then paused. He glared at the android. "Well?"

The disfigured, hulking thing spoke. "She will be fine. I've scanned her entire body the way you requested. The trauma to her head is the worst of it and there is no internal cranial bleeding or swelling. She will have a lump and I estimate the probability of a headache when she wakes. With your permission, I'll give her an injection for the pain she should experience upon waking and a few hours beyond."

"Do it." Zorus then turned to glower at Sky who stood at attention just inside the door. "You can live."

Sky frowned but then his body relaxed. "I'm sorry. How the hell could I have known you had grown soft over a woman?"

"Don't make me regret not killing you."

The cyborg grinned. "I can't believe you're fond of a human. I take it Earth turned into an ice ball?"

"What does that mean?" He longed to punch Sky again.

"Hell froze over."

"Get out."

Zorus watched Sky leave and turned back in time to witness the android give Charlie an injection to her hip. The thing moved forward and then paused.

"Is that all?"

"Leave," Zorus ordered, detesting the android that had come with the ship but grateful it had medical training. "Thank you."

It rambled out of the room to leave him alone with Charlie. She could have been killed when she'd grabbed hold of a weapon. She didn't trust him and that made his level of fury notch higher. She'd been hurt, something he hadn't meant to do, when he'd disarmed her but he'd taken advantage of her distraction. It could have ended far worse. No one had died and her head injury wasn't life threatening. He moved to stand at the side of the bed.

He hesitated and then sat on the side of the mattress to hold her limp hand. He closed his eyes and allowed his feelings to surface. He could have lost her. It really made him angry and he didn't want to part with her. She had heard Sky, obviously believed he'd tricked her with deceit and he guessed she wouldn't trust him easily again.

She'll try to escape. That's what I would do but I won't allow it.

He carefully placed her hand over her stomach before he stood. His gaze drifted around the captain's quarters. The room belonged to the human woman whom Coal had claimed. He searched it quickly and found some stretchy material. To keep Charlie unconscious with drugs wasn't a possibility he wanted to consider with her head injury. He approached the bed.

"I'm sorry," he whispered. "You're going to have to learn to trust me again."

Regret wasn't something he experienced often but he did when he gently undressed her. Charlie never stirred, which worried him, but he didn't hesitate to finish what he'd started. He secured her to the bed, covered her with a blanket to keep her warm, and then connected with the ship's computer. He sent a message to one of the three androids that cared for the shuttle.

Minutes later food arrived. Zorus studied the android that brought it. "Thank you."

"No problem," it stated. "Is there anything else you need?"

"No. I'll let you know if there is. Tell my comrades I don't want to be disturbed."

"I will relay the message."

Zorus stepped back with the tray in hand and then sealed the doors to lock them from the inside. He disconnected his link to the onboard computer after making sure they were on their way to the *Star*. He wanted to return to Garden as quickly as possible.

His gaze drifted to the sleeping woman on the bed. She wouldn't be happy with his plans for her but she'd have to adjust. Humans were capable of adapting. He placed the tray on the floor since the room didn't contain a table. He returned to the bed to ease his weight down. His mind ran the variables of how she'd react when she woke while he watched her sleep.

* * * * *

When Charlie regained consciousness, she felt a bit lightheaded and confused. She opened her eyes and stared up at an unfamiliar ceiling but the metal beams told her she had to be on a ship. Memory slowly surfaced and she tried to sit but her arms and legs were held immobile. She wondered if she'd been drugged again but then lifted her head. The room wasn't a large one, feminine things adorned shelves, and then it all came back. They'd boarded a shuttle with cyborgs and a human woman. Zorus had fought with his own men and he'd fooled her into believing he had a decent side.

The door located in the corner opened and she stared with trepidation at the cyborg who stepped into the room wearing nothing but a small towel around his waist. His hair dripped from the cleansing unit and water drops slid down his impressive chest. His dark gaze immediately locked on her.

"I hurried in hopes I'd be out before you woke."

She attempted to move again but something kept her restrained. She had to twist her head to see material wrapped tightly around both wrists, secured to the top of the bed frame, her arms above her head. Zorus moved closer.

"I apologize for tying you but I feared you'd attack again. I didn't want to risk you being injured twice. You will be fine."

The glare she shot him made him take a step back. "Let me go."

"I'm not going to do that." Zorus took a deep breath. "You're safe with me, Charlie. What you heard about me isn't completely true. Do you remember my explanation about the humans I befriended and then had to kill?"

"You said they were bounty hunters."

"They were. Rumors of cyborgs in space have circulated for years and occasionally they travel too close to the planet we settled on, looking for signs of us. We have sent ships out to capture them, taken them to Garden—that's our planet—and then had to learn what they knew. We left Earth to avoid a war with Earth Government. We just want to live in peace."

"I heard something about cyborgs owning humans too and you're responsible for that."

His mouth tensed into a tight line before he spoke. "That is true. Cyborgs were considered property by Earth Government on your planet. I believed it would be fitting to turn the tables on your kind. Cyborgs own humans where I live."

"You bought me from that captain and now you think you own me."

It hurt her to even say it, the betrayal a wound inside her heart put there by the man she'd allowed to make love to her. She'd even gone down on him because she'd wanted to make him happy when he'd been grumpy. It had all been a lie on his behalf. He'd used her just to distract her from escaping the shuttle so he could keep her long enough to do this to her.

"I feel so stupid. I assumed you'd done it out of the goodness of your heart when I heard you'd paid that captain to save me from Gerald getting his hands on me." She looked at the chest she'd used for a pillow the night before and then looked back up into his eyes. "I guess you don't have one of those, do you?"

"Charlie…" He moved closer.

"Don't you dare," she yelled. "I won't be a whore to any man. Do you hear me? I won't be forced to have sex with some asshole who thinks he's got a right to hurt me because money exchanged hands."

Anger darkened his features when he sat on the edge of the bed near her hip. "I'm not asking you to be a whore, nor would I force you to have intercourse with me." He paused. "I wouldn't make you fuck me. I paid for your release to keep you out of the hands of the human but I had none of the motives at the time that you believe me guilty of. You are unique and I wanted to pay you back for being concerned for my welfare."

She wanted to believe him badly. "Then why am I tied to a bed?" She shifted her hips and her bare skin touched the sheet. "Naked."

"You believe I kill humans for fun and that I lured you onto this ship to kill you as well."

She couldn't deny that. "Your own cyborgs don't like you, do they?"

"No." He looked miserable as he spoke. "The ones on this shuttle do not. The only one who doesn't hold a grudge against me would be Coal, the bald one. I haven't done anything to anger him yet."

She noticed the "yet". "Why do they hate you?"

He paused before he drew in a deep breath. "I believed humans who entered into family units with cyborgs were detrimental to my species. I didn't understand why any of our males would choose one of you over one of our own females. I attempted to block them from cementing their unions."

"You wanted those women killed." It wasn't a question, more of a statement since she knew deep down that he had. She'd heard as much.

"Yes."

It still horrified her to hear him admit it. She had to look away from his face and focus on the drops of water near his nipple. "What are you going to do with me?"

"I shielded you with my body and ordered my men to stand down when you held a weapon. Think logically. If I wished your death I wouldn't have done that."

She met his calm stare. "You want to kill me yourself?"

Anger tightened his handsome face. "No. I won't allow any harm to come to you."

He looked sincere and she felt confused. "Then what do you want?"

He leaned closer, put his hand on the other side of the bed by her hip, and the look on his face softened. "I wish you would trust that I don't hate you, nor do I want anything to happen to you."

"Why?"

"You make me feel, Charlie. For the first time in my life, logic doesn't apply foremost. I don't know why I'm so attracted to you or what causes the emotions that arise inside me but I want to continue our relationship to figure it out. I have chosen not to fight it." He paused. "What about you? Are you willing to see how this is going to play out between us?"

Sincerity sounded in his voice. He either could really act or he told her the truth. The confused look on his features tended to make her believe him. He wasn't masking his emotions now, rather allowing her to see them.

"What if we do this and you decide humans really are detrimental to cyborgs? I'm not really sure what your version of that is but what does my future hold if you get sick of me in a week or two? What happens when we argue? I'm not always exactly easy to get along with. If you think I'm going to bow to your will, rethInk it."

A small smile flashed. "I actually enjoy it when you are irritating me, for the most part." Serious again, he leaned forward until only inches separated their faces. "We'll make a pact. I swear to protect you from all harm, even from my own hand, if you swear not to attempt to escape my care."

"And if I want to leave later?"

He hesitated. "I want to be completely honest with you."

A sense of dread gripped her. "I wish you would be."

"It would be too risky to allow you to visit Garden, my planet, and then release you. You would have knowledge that could harm my people."

"You're saying you won't let me go, aren't you?"

His hand rose and he brushed back hair from her cheek, his fingertips a soft caress on her skin. "I won't force sex on you or make you live inside my home but you won't be allowed to leave Garden."

"I'll be a slave to someone else?"

"No. I give you my word that you will live in peace, free from harm, regardless of what happens between us. Earth Government will be hunting for you and we both know Saturn isn't far enough away for them not to track you there if they really want you in their custody. They will never find you on my planet. You'll be much safer on Garden than anywhere else."

"But Russell has all my money. I need to go after him. All I own are the clothes on my back." She fought tears. "I don't even have those anymore."

"You won't need money where we're going, Charlie. I'll provide you with all that you could ask for."

"So I'll be your kept woman?" Anger and pain burned inside her chest. "That's a whore. You'll be giving me money and things in exchange for sex."

"I'm taking you from everything you know to force you to live on a planet unfamiliar to you. The sex is optional and only if you want to share it with me. I'll be compensating you for bringing you into my world."

She closed her eyes and turned her head. "My head hurts and I'm still tired. May I be alone?"

110

The silence grew very uncomfortable, only broken by their breathing. The bed finally moved when Zorus rose to his feet.

"I'll get dressed and leave you to rest. Please consider my offer, Charlie. It is a genuine one. You can trust me."

Zorus left her alone after he dressed. As soon as the door closed behind his retreating body, she stared at the metal door. Hot tears blinded her and she tugged at the bindings that held her down. He hadn't untied her, hadn't trusted her not to try to escape, and she knew then he really was intelligent. Escape would be her first option if given the chance.

"Damn you, Russell, you piece of shit," she sniffed. "This is totally your fault. You had to screw up what we had on Earth and look where I am now."

She pulled harder on the restraints, watched the material go taut where it secured her to the bed, but it didn't break. She tried to jerk her legs up but Zorus had tied something around her ankles, her legs spread wide open under the thick, warm comforter shielding her body. She twisted and fought until she grew exhausted.

Chapter Seven

Zorus entered the room hours later only to find Charlie sleeping again. He moved soundlessly across the room to stare down at her. He noticed the tracks on the sides of her face where her tears had streamed but then dried. The bedding covering her revealed the struggle she'd put up, the once-smooth surface now a mess of wrinkles. His saw slightly reddened skin around her wrists. His jaw clenched. *Damn stubborn female.*

He turned to place another tray of food on the floor with the hope that he could talk her into eating. He'd never been responsible for someone's care before. He didn't believe his skills were lacking until he'd met the fascinating human. His gaze returned to her and the shape of her body barely concealed beneath the blankets. He muffled a groan that threatened to rise when his body responded to the tempting sight.

She'd have to learn to trust that he had no ill will toward her and only wanted them to be as they had been the night before. He bent down to tear off his boots. Frustration nearly boiled over as he straightened then reached for his shirt. He wanted Charlie yet didn't know how to make her yearn for his touch.

The shirt dropped to the floor and he unfastened his pants. His cock sprang free when he pushed them down his hips. He glared at the part of his body that seemed to have ruled his brain for the past twenty-four hours. Memories of Charlie in his arms made his cock swell harder, longer, and he softly cursed under his breath.

He paced, occasionally glancing at the sleeping woman, his mind going over feasible scenarios on the fastest way to alleviate her worries over his long-term intentions. He paused when an idea struck. Humans were needier than cyborgs. They placed a lot of trust in set roles inside their society. He discarded the idea almost as quickly as it struck. She'd be even more suspicious if he offered her too much, too fast.

Charlie moved in her sleep, her back arched, and a soft moan came from her parted lips. He froze and watched her wiggle her hips, noticed her faster breathing, and flushed features. A slow grin spread as he inched closer to the bed. She dreamed and he had a good idea where it had led.

He'd be a bastard for taking advantage of the situation. *Then again*, he reasoned silently, *she already believes I'm one.*

He reached for the bedding to slowly pull it down her body to reveal every seductive inch of her pale, creamy body. It took his breath away to see her stretched out naked, bound, and spread open. His gaze traveled from her wrists to the vee of her thighs where proof gleamed wetly that her sleeping mind had gone where he'd hoped it had.

He debated for a long minute but then she tossed her head, another moan passed her lips, and his cock twitched painfully, aching for the woman who had become his sole focus, and probably the beginning of an addiction. His knee gently dipped the mattress when he climbed onto it with her. He tried not to wake her when he unbound each ankle. *The worst that could happen is that she will be very angry when she wakes up...but she already is.*

Charlie arched her hips to seek the hot, wet, wonderful sensation that rasped across her clit. She ached badly, desire burning throughout her body, and the heels of her feet dug into something warm, solid, and fleshy. Firm hands pushed her thighs wider apart and something tickled the skin there as well but nothing distracted from the constant flicking against her throbbing clit.

"Yes," she moaned, bucking her hips.

She had to be dreaming about Zorus. No man had ever made her feel the way he could. She opened her eyes to stare in a passion-filled daze at the ceiling and the sensation only grew stronger. She hovered on the edge of climax, ready to beg if need be to get there.

She lifted her head to peer down over her stomach to watch a dark head and broad shoulders between her spread thighs, her legs bent up around his upper arms, and her heels rested on the top of his shoulder blades. Zorus suckled her clit, tugged on it, and his tongue swiped across the swollen, throbbing bud again.

"Faster," she whispered. "Please, Zorus?"

He groaned, the deep sound vibrated against her clit, and his mouth tugged harder, his tongue doing things to her that nearly hurt—the pleasure was that intense and raw. Her body arched up again to press her hips tighter against his face and that did it. Charlie screamed out when the orgasm gripped her and shot her into sheer bliss that threatened to steal not only her ability to think but to breathe.

Her eyes were closed and she panted. Her vaginal walls twitched hard, aching to be filled. *Hell of a dream*. It had seemed so real, still did when the

114

bed shifted and her heels slid down his back while he shrugged them aside. She opened her eyes and watched him crawl higher over her body. His dark eyes looked black in the dim room and happened to be the sexiest things she'd ever seen. His handsome face seemed a darker, duskier color, and his generous lips looked a little swollen to her, puffy, and she wanted to kiss them.

"You're so beautiful," he rasped softly.

His body lowered, his chest pressed tightly to hers, nearly crushing her taut nipples against his hot skin. They lay stomach to stomach, his face hovering mere inches over her own.

"Tell me 'no' if you don't want me."

She tried to touch his face but her arms wouldn't work. The dream turned to frustration for an instant and then his gaze narrowed. Zorus softly groaned when the broad, hard tip of his cock nudged her very slick, ready pussy. The instant he started to enter her, stretch her, reality slammed home. His mouth crushed down over hers to capture the moan he drew from her when he filled her. His cock reminded her of steel and pleasure blinded her while he made her body take all of his thick cock. He held still there and then his tongue slid between her parted lips.

She could taste herself on his tongue, not an unpleasant thing, and then he growled loudly and started to rock his hips, to fuck her deeply and steadily. Her muscles gripped his driving cock, fluttered from the aftermath of her climax, and she wanted to cry out from the way it made her pleasure rise higher to draw out the orgasm that still resonated.

Sensory overload enthralled her, from his hungry mouth dominating hers and his powerful body that took her harder and faster as his hips hammered her into the soft mattress without mercy. Her erect, sensitive nipples rubbed against his chest and with the angle he had on her hips, his groin rubbed against her swollen, oversensitive clit. Even having her arms tied above her head notched the level of sexual tension. She came again, bucked against his body frantically, and cried out against his tongue.

Zorus tore his mouth from hers, threw his head back, and roared out her name while his body jerked violently. His semen spread warmth deep inside her pussy while his cock throbbed as if it had a heartbeat against her convulsing vaginal walls. He braced his arms to keep from totally collapsing on top of her chest when his body sagged until he stilled over her.

Charlie turned her head, panted, and closed her eyes. That had been no dream. It may have started out as one but somewhere along the way it had become reality. Zorus lowered his head, his mouth brushing a kiss on the side of her throat, and then his lips parted, so his tongue could trace the vein he found. She shivered with erotic delight at the soft touch.

"Promise me you won't try to escape. I want your hands on me."

She hated how badly she wanted to say yes. She bit her lip. Zorus softly cursed and kissed her throat again, this time harder, and his cock flexed inside her. It amazed her that he remained hard after coming. She knew he had since there was no missing the heated warmth and she guessed his hotter body temperature accounted for that.

"Please," his voice turned husky when he spoke against her throat. "Just promise me for now."

That she could do. "Yes."

His mouth left her and he lifted off her a little. Charlie turned her head and watched him reach up with one hand. He grabbed the material above her wrists and gave a mighty tug to easily tear it from the frame of the bed. It showed her how strong he was since she sure hadn't been able to do that.

He gripped one wrist and brought it to his mouth. He used his teeth to untie the knots and free her. He turned his head and dropped the material from his mouth then frowned when he saw the skin that he had uncovered.

"You mark so easily. I'm sorry."

Their gazes met and she could see the truth lurking in his eyes. "It doesn't hurt. Whatever you used didn't tighten on my skin and it's soft."

"I believe they are leggings, belonging to the human who normally occupies this room."

Charlie turned her arm, twisting a little, and Zorus released his hold on it. She slowly lowered her arm until her palm rested on his biceps. She loved to touch him, to feel his smooth, strong body, and the heat he generated.

"The other one, please."

He nodded and then shifted his gaze from her to free her other wrist. She gripped both his arms. Zorus lowered back on top of her, braced his elbows on the mattress next to her ribs, and effectively caged her under his body. Their gazes met again and held as effectively as their bodies were connected.

"Please don't attack me, Charlie. I won't hurt you but I don't want to tie you again."

"I'm not stupid. You're too strong and fast. I saw you fight with that other cyborg inside the cargo hold and I'll never forget how easily you snapped that dock worker's neck. I wouldn't stand a chance."

He actually flinched. "I don't want you to fear me. I'd never use my strength to harm you."

"Just to tie me to a bed and seduce me when I'm half asleep."

Guilt passed over his handsome features. "I'll take you any way I can get you. Do you hate me for admitting that?"

She actually didn't. "At least you're being honest. You get points for that."

"Points?" His eyebrows arched. "What does that mean?"

The humor struck her, Zorus had a way of doing that to her sometimes with his lack of basic slang terms, and she smiled against her will. "It means I have to respect you for telling the truth. The points thing is just a saying."

"I'll make note of that for future reference."

She flat out grinned.

"What is so amusing?" He looked anything but amused with that befuddled expression that she found so cute on him.

"You're showing your computer side again."

"I'm not familiar with Earth sayings any longer and admit it wasn't my strong suit even when I lived there."

"I bet. It's all about logic with you."

"Not all." He took a deep breath, nearly crushed her chest under his, but then adjusted his body a little higher to ease his weight from pressing too hard against her. "There's nothing logical about my reactions to you. I'm…" He didn't continue.

Curiosity gripped Charlie. She rubbed his arms, tracing upward to the curve of his shoulders. "You're what? Talk to me."

"I've entirely evaluated my reactions to you. I'm displaying possessive, bordering on obsessive, behavior that isn't within my normal range of emotions. You make me feel unfamiliar sentiments, Charlie. I'm not certain how to proceed with them, but regardless of my inability to control them, I refuse to suppress them. You make me take risks I never believed I would be capable of. Even telling you all of my uncertainties is against my normal personality traits. I am usually very guarded with my thoughts."

"I'm glad you're talking to me." She continued to run her fingertips along his skin, realizing she could touch him for hours and never get tired of it.

"Tell me what thoughts and emotions you are experiencing." He hesitated. "Please."

She swallowed and then took a deep breath. "I'm confused. You do that to me. I didn't like you at all when we first met. You were ice cold and a real asshole, if you want the truth. When we're in bed together you're softer and a lot easier to like."

His features hardened and all emotion cleared. "That's all you feel for me? A *like* of the fucking we do together?"

She studied him carefully and saw a hint of anger brewing. He tried to hide it but the more time they spent together, he became easier for her to read. The darkening in color of his eyes—quickly turning nearly black—gave him away. She tried to form her words carefully.

"If that is all that is between us, I'll order them to pilot us to the nearest station where you can obtain passage to Saturn." He tried to lift off her.

Charlie's fingernails dug into his skin to grasp hold of his shoulders. "Freeze."

He stopped moving and his mouth tightened into an angry line. Fury radiated from his gaze, clearly now. *Oh yeah*, she realized. *He's really pissed and maybe even hurt.* It surprised her that she could make him feel that much so fast.

"I won't force you to stay with me just for the sake of good intercourse."

She noticed he'd changed back to the habit of calling sex between them the colder term instead of saying fucking. He'd at least made an effort to call it something she'd suggested, a fact she'd taken note of.

"I said I'm confused. We just met and I've never gone to bed with a man so fast. I'm feeling more for you than just the physical stuff we do. I'm just afraid to trust you and I don't know if we're too different to try to have any kind of lasting relationship. We're moving way too fast and after what my brother did to me, and my ex-lover, can you see why I don't trust my own judgment when it comes to guys I'm drawn to? I want to trust you but your own cyborgs don't like you. That's screaming a warning signal inside my head that I'm going to get hurt."

"I promised you no harm."

"I'm not talking about you hitting me or killing me. Sure, I'm apprehensive about that a little but mostly I'm worried about getting attached to you and then you figuring out I'm just a passing itch you wanted to scratch."

His body relaxed again over hers and his weight settled down. "I am not experiencing any physical irritations when we are together."

A laugh came from her easily. "It's another saying. I don't mean I'm giving you a rash. I meant that sometimes physical attraction fades and then what would we have? You'd move on to someone else. You're asking me to go live in a world that I'm pretty certain isn't going to be friendly to a woman from Earth. I'll be stuck there without a way to leave. What am I supposed to do when you dump me?"

"I've estimated the odds and the cyborg males who have joined with humans haven't lost their attraction to each other." He licked his lips. "If anything they seem to grow closer and get even more attached to one another."

"What if we don't?"

"There are no guarantees I can give you accurately. I could lie to you by doing so but I don't want deceit between us. The odds for survival of a long-lasting relationship built on distrust and falsehoods are very low."

Charlie had to admit that his total honesty drew her to him even more. "You won't lie to me then?"

"You have my word of honor. I will always tell you completely honest answers if I'm able to."

"What does that mean?"

"As a councilman there will be information I learn that will be labeled classified. I won't be permitted to share that with you even if we ever become joined in a family unit. I won't lie to you but I will tell you if I'm unable to answer."

"I can deal with that." She smiled. "I meant about the things between us."

"I give you my word of honor. You can depend on that always."

She believed him. "What is 'joined as a family unit'?"

Zorus remained silent.

"Is that classified information?"

"No."

"Then what does it mean?"

"It's our version of marriage."

"And why don't you want to talk about it? I don't expect you to marry me now. We barely know each other. I just want to know what it is since you brought it up." A horrible thought struck. "Are you married?"

"No." He didn't look away from her. "I was joined in a family unit but no longer."

Charlie barely refrained from wincing. The idea of Zorus married to someone else wasn't one she enjoyed imagining. He'd said he wasn't married anymore. "She died or you divorced?"

"We mutually ended the contract."

"She couldn't take how cold you are, could she?" It was a good guess on Charlie's part.

"My emotional disconnection had nothing to do with the dissolution of the contract."

"Then why did you divorce?"

"I'm sterile so I didn't feel the need to remain with her after it became clear we didn't enjoy spending any time together." He glanced away from her and then back. "I mentioned that to you before. I will never be able to give you children from my sperm. The only way for you to breed would be if you accepted another male into our family unit with active, viable sperm."

"Come again?" Charlie gaped at him.

"You want sex already? I thought it best to give you a reasonable resting time since you're not as physically resilient as cyborg females."

His misunderstanding of slang wasn't funny to her this time. "What do you mean, accept another male into a family unit?"

He didn't speak.

"Zorus? Talk to me."

"I don't wish to give you that information."

"Why?" She tensed. Their rules and his world were different from Earth's. She didn't need to be a scholar to get that. Whatever he wasn't saying had to be something so bad he feared she'd bolt. "I need the truth here."

Anger flashed in his eyes. "I don't want another male to touch you."

"I don't want that either."

He studied her carefully, seemed to look for something, perhaps trying to tell if she was lying. He finally spoke. "There are far less female cyborgs than males. We had to make adjustments to form family units accordingly."

"Speak English or expand on the explanation because I'm not getting it."

"Our males share a single female when they form a family unit."

Shock rolled through Charlie. "Then we sure as hell won't be getting married."

"That wouldn't be an issue unless you demanded children. Even as my property, you could force the issue by demanding another male enter into our family unit to provide them. I'm unable to breed children with you, which would mean a viable male could be brought into our family unit if you asked. All cyborg family units must produce at least one child per each member—cyborg member—and given that law, if you agreed to be a breeder for a male it would override my rights to sole ownership of you in a family-unit situation."

Charlie knew her mouth hung open but for the life of her she couldn't close it. Zorus frowned down at her with a decidedly unhappy grimace. The astonishment started to fade and she cleared her throat, licked her lips, and managed to stop gaping at him.

"I'm not a slut. I don't cheat either. I've never done two guys at once and never would. That's just wrong. My parents raised me not to be immoral."

"It is not considered promiscuous on Garden for a woman to have many males in her family unit." He paused. "That term I am familiar with.

124

A female is not a slut if she has multiple males in a family unit. She's giving the males the opportunity to create life, give our race a future, and she is revered."

"I'm not from Garden and I sure as hell don't need more than one man in my life."

"Do you give me your word of honor on that?" Hope flared in his gaze.

"Yes," she promised with all sincerity. "I'm not a cheater and in my book that's what it would be. I wouldn't ever want more than one man in my life."

"Good. We're in total agreement that no other male shall ever touch you regardless of my inability to breed children with you."

She nodded. "We are."

He hesitated. "I have a son."

The shocks kept coming for Charlie. "You had a kid and then decided not to have any more? You asked to be sterilized?"

"He was created before I escaped Earth. He's the product of the testing the scientists forced on my people to see if we could breed. I got a female cyborg pregnant. I told you that once it had been established that it was possible, they sterilized the males to prevent our future breeding. Some of their options were medically reversible. In my case the damage is permanent. When I escaped, I took my son with me."

"Where is his mother?" Jealousy surfaced though she tried not to feel it. The idea of him having a son with another woman didn't sit well with her.

"I took her to Garden as well. I wasn't about to leave her behind. We formed a family unit for the sake of our child but we did not tolerate one another in the least. It is why we mutually ended the contract."

"How long ago was that?"

"Fifteen years have passed since the contract ended."

She let go of the green-eyed monster. Fifteen years was a really long time and he hadn't said it but she got the feeling that he and his ex-wife hated each other. "Do you see her often?"

"No. We avoid common meeting areas."

"Even better," she muttered.

Zorus suddenly smiled. "You do not enjoy the idea of me spending time with her?"

"No and I don't see what is so amusing to you about that."

"Jealousy is a first-level emotion of a growing attachment."'

"I'm so happy that you're thrilled over that." She didn't roll her eyes but she wanted to. "Note my sarcastic tone."

He had the audacity to chuckle. "You are feeling deeper feelings for me than just sexual gratification."

There wasn't a reason to deny it. "Yes but I'm still really confused. I don't know what I'm getting into and I'm not sure this is such a hot idea. What happens if we don't work out? I'll be stuck on this cyborg planet of yours, correct?"

"I'm determined to make our relationship a solid, happy union that will last."

"Relationships aren't that simple."

Zorus kept his smile in place. "You will learn I am a very stubborn male who has little to no sway in my directives."

"That's what scares me."

Chapter Eight

Charlie couldn't stop staring at the buildings and how uniform in shape they were. It appeared as if they'd used the same blueprint to construct each one. The streets were so clean, she guessed someone could actually eat off them. She also didn't miss the way heads turned to openly study her. She inched closer to Zorus to grab his hand in a tight grip.

He paused, his gaze lowered to her hand clutching his. He met her gaze with concern. "There is no need to be afraid. No harm will come to you here, Charlie."

"I don't see any humans," she whispered, not wanting anyone nearby to overhear her. "Please tell me I'm not the only one on this planet. When you said humans were slaves I assumed I'd see a bunch of them."

"You are not the only one but there are very few."

"That doesn't reassure me at all. Does every cyborg hate me for being human? I'm not seeing any happy faces."

Zorus peered around them. "It's irrelevant what their personal opinions of humans are. You are safe with me. No one would dare attempt to harm you."

"They are staring at me."

"You're a rarity." He paused. "It might be the surprise of seeing me with a human that holds their fascination more. It's well-known that I abhor everything from Earth."

She inched closer until her body pressed against his side. "You mean you used to feel that way."

"Yes." He grinned. "You are the only thing from Earth that makes it a relevant place. Would you prefer I carry you? You could turn your face against my chest and not look at them if they frighten you. I could easily do that without straining my body. You're quite light to me."

"I'm not a baby." Her chin lifted and she stepped away. "I'd like to keep hold of your hand if you don't mind though."

He gave her hand a gentle squeeze. "My home is just two buildings down on the right side. We'll be out of their sight soon. You'll be more comfortable without their scrutiny."

"Good. Lead the way."

It took a lot for her not to ask Zorus to carry her. She couldn't miss how many cyborgs openly watched her with grim looks. Some came outside the buildings they passed to do so, and she didn't see any sign of welcome when she dared glance at faces. With every step, she bumped into Zorus. She remained that close to his side.

He entered a building, nodded to a guard, and led her to an elevator. The second it opened, Charlie nearly leaped inside the empty lift. Zorus frowned at her but followed her in. The doors sealed them inside.

"You are safe, Charlie."

"Safe but really uncomfortable. I think I know how a dangerous animal at the zoo feels now. Everyone out there looked as if I were a snake, or something equally as unpleasant, about to strike out at them."

His features tensed. "I will do something about that. I'll order them not to stare at you the next time we go out."

Surprised, she studied him closely and asked, "You could do that?"

He gave a sharp nod. "I'm a council member. My opinion matters to all and I can be very persuasive."

She had heard the cyborgs call him that but hadn't let it sink in what it could possibly mean. "You're a bigwig on this planet?"

"I don't understand the term but I am an important, ruling member of the cyborg council. I help create the laws for our people and judge when someone breaks those laws. If I issue an order it will be followed."

She shook her head, her gaze lowering to his leather-clad chest. "Don't sweat it. I'll adjust. I don't want anyone resenting me right off the bat if you order them to be nice to me."

"I don't understand."

She smiled when she stepped closer to him. Her hands touched the material of his shirt, enjoying the feel but she preferred to feel his skin. "I don't want to make waves or have your people dislike me because you tell them to do the opposite."

His hands encased her hips. "You make no sense."

Her hands rubbed the leather. "Does everyone here wear this stuff? I noticed most of you do."

"Not all."

"Where do you get leather on this planet anyway?"

"It's synthetic. There are plants that grow here that have the same texture and we've managed to harvest them to make clothing. When the plant is cut it hardens, blackens, yet still keeps some elasticity. It's blended with a gluey substance that keeps the fibers connected. We have become self-sufficient on Garden. The only thing we can't obtain here are metals. We do a lot of trading and salvaging to obtain those."

The doors opened and Zorus released her, turned, and grabbed her hand. "This is my floor."

He meant that literally, she discovered when they exited the elevator. It didn't open up into a corridor but instead into a huge living area. She gawked at the sheer size of his quarters. It had to be the largest she'd ever seen. Tasteful furniture decorated the vast area. The view from the large walls of windows revealed that they were probably on the top floor of the building.

She released his hand, moved across the room to a window, and stared out at the city below. A large wall rose in the distance, and then beyond that trees ended where a blue ocean stretched as far as she could see. The view was breathtaking.

"It's lovely."

Zorus moved behind her and his arms wrapped around her body to pull her back against his chest. "I told you it would somewhat resemble Earth. It's good to be home."

His home, not mine. At least not yet. A hundred questions filled her mind and she turned in his arms to peer up at his handsome face. She didn't miss the smile while he continued to gaze over her head at the view behind her.

"You love it here," she surmised.

His gaze met hers. "Yes. We are at peace. I am proud we've accomplished so much. When we first arrived we had to live on our ships. It took a lot of years to build the walls to encase our city. Once we secured the area we were able to concentrate our efforts on creating our homes."

"You should be proud. It's really beautiful and so clean." She flashed back to the memory of their streets. "Do cyborgs get along well?"

"There is no crime if that is what you wish to know. We are happy to have our freedom, our society is well-established, and we base our lives on logic."

It sounded a little cold to her but she didn't know enough to judge their society. Zorus turned her inside the circle of his arms to face the window again. She leaned back against his chest, content with the view he seemed to enjoy, and she couldn't fault him for it. Garden was beautiful.

"I don't want to leave the surface again. My days of traveling out into space aren't as tempting as they used to be. I never believed I'd see home again."

Her heart wrenched a little at the sadness she heard in his voice but she was also reminded that she'd never see her home again. Earth wasn't as perfect as the view before her but it was all she'd known.

His hold around her waist tightened into a hug. "You will be happy here, Charlie. I will make certain of it."

She turned her head to look up at him, met his gaze, and smiled. "I hope so. You did promise."

"I keep my word."

"Don't tense up on me. I was teasing." Her attention drifted to the room. "Wow, is this place huge. Is it all yours?"

He turned her to face the room. "The entire floor is our home."

She liked how he'd corrected her from his to theirs. "How many bedrooms do we have?"

"Four. They are all quite comfortable."

"I hope you don't expect me to clean all this." She chuckled. "I'm not real good at that and don't pull maid duty well."

"Others are assigned to that task." His hold loosened. "You are not my slave." His voice hardened. "Look at me."

She turned to face him again. "I was just joking, trying to break the tension. I don't—"

Zorus' mouth descended over hers to cut off her words. His hold on her adjusted and he lifted her against his body until her feet left the floor. Charlie wrapped her arms around his neck and her legs around his hips. Desire for the tall cyborg flared instantly to life. The man turned her on like no other man ever had. She kissed him back. He moved but she didn't care where he took her as long as their lips didn't separate.

He eased her down on something soft and big, released her, and backed away. She smiled when he tore at his shirt then glanced around the big bedroom he'd carried her into. The room had one solid-glass wall with no curtains, the view similar to the one from the living room, and it had to be the biggest sleeping quarters she'd ever seen. Her entire apartment could have fit inside it.

"This is our bedroom," he informed her while he bent to tear off his boots. "Strip."

The massive bed barely moved when she climbed off to remove her shoes and her clothes. "In a hurry, Zorus?"

"Yes." He didn't bother to hide that fact when he jerked his pants down his hips to reveal every hard inch of his incredibly sexy body. "I have to leave soon but wish to touch you before I have a council meeting."

She undressed, sat on the edge of the bed, and stared up at him. "Am I going with you?"

He shook his head and inched closer to her until his hips were in front of her face. She smiled when she lowered her gaze down his muscled abs to the thick, hard cock protruding inches from her mouth.

"Want me to do something in particular?" She reached up, her fingertips stroked the stiff, aroused flesh of his shaft, and she grinned when it jerked in reaction to the light trace of her touch.

"Will you take me inside your mouth again? I enjoyed that immensely."

Charlie licked her lips and opened her mouth. Zorus gasped in air when she wrapped her mouth around the crown of his cock. She tasted that sweet flavor his pre-cum carried, and moaned her enjoyment. She'd never really liked giving head much but Zorus wasn't typical in any sense. He'd also gone down on her, seemingly happy to do it, and the memory of what his mouth could do turned her on.

She took him deeper inside her mouth to suck and lick him. She tensed a bit when his hand slid into her hair to curl his fingers around the back of her head but he didn't try to force her closer to take more of his length than she could handle. Instead he just loosely held on to her, his fingers massaging her scalp, and allowed her to move how she wanted. Soft groans came from the sexy cyborg.

She lowered her hand down her body, her knees spread, and her fingers slid through the wetness of her own arousal. She ached for him but didn't want to stop since he seemed to love what her mouth did to him. She teased her clit, rubbed in slow circles, and moaned louder from the self-induced pleasure.

"Charlie," he rasped. "I smell you and want a taste. Release me."

She sucked him a little harder, knew from how unbelievably hard he'd grown—soft, velvety steel against her tongue—that he would come at any second. The fingers tangled in her hair tightened before he tugged her head back. She cried out in protest from being forced away from his cock and from the slight pain he caused.

Zorus dropped to his knees on the plush carpet between her spread legs, released her hair, and gripped her thighs. Charlie gasped when she suddenly ended up on her back with her thighs shoved up into the air. Zorus spread her wider, his strong hands easily manipulated her position, and he buried his face against her pussy.

His aggressive mouth attacked, nothing gentle about the way his tongue plowed against the sensitive, swollen bud she'd been playing with, or how he sealed his mouth around it to tug on it and create a hard suction.

Charlie cried out, clawed his red, silky bedspread, and arched her hips closer to his amazing mouth. Her feet ended up dangling down his back and she used the leverage to press her pussy even tighter against his unrelenting mouth. The ecstasy was so intense that she couldn't breathe. She panted and gasped instead, between broken moans.

"Zorus! Yes! Don't stop. Please? Oh god!" The climax built, hovered, and she cried out in anguish when he tore his mouth away.

Her eyes flew open to protest but she watched him straighten, let her legs to drop to spread around his hips when his hands left her thighs, and then the broad head of his cock pushed against her vagina. He snarled at her, his features a mask of passion, and then they both cried out when he entered her fast and deep. His thick cock slid into her, stretched her vaginal walls fast, nerve endings shot pure rapture to her brain at the tight fit their bodies created.

One of his hands flattened on her lower stomach to hold her down while he started to move, fucking her hard and deep, and to notch up the pleasure his thumb hooked over her pelvic bone to press against her clit. His other hand gripped one of her thighs to jerk it up to his ribs to hold her in place. He pounded against her, drove in and out of her with wild abandon, and Charlie flew apart from the pleasure of him riding her with his cock and her clit with his thumb, the combination making her come hard enough to convulse and scream.

Zorus roared out her name, his hold on her became almost bruising while his hips jerked. His hot semen shot deep inside her and Charlie felt every blast. Her vaginal walls milked him in the aftermath of her volatile climax. They stilled except for their racing hearts and ragged breathing. Charlie smiled when she opened her eyes again to meet his passionate gaze. He licked his lips, sweat beaded his brow and upper lip, and a slow, satisfied grin curved that mouth she couldn't get enough of.

"You will live with me here, won't you?"

She'd forgotten he'd given her a choice, once mentioning he wouldn't make her share his home if she didn't want to. "If this is part of the benefits living with you entails, try to make me leave." She grinned. "You live here alone, don't you?"

He nodded. "My place in cyborg society offers me a penthouse suite." He slowly withdrew from her body but leaned down to stretch over her until they were nearly nose to nose. "I am happy that you prefer to stay with me and I hope to share this room. There are guestrooms if you prefer." His features seemed to harden. "I want you in here with me, if you care to know my preference."

"I enjoyed sleeping with you," she admitted.

He grinned and all traces of unhappiness faded away. "I enjoyed it as well. It's settled. We share a bed every night."

She wasn't sure what to say. Zorus drew back. "I must shower and be on time for the council meeting. Make yourself familiar with our home."

She hated it when he stood and turned away from her, but liked the nice view of his beefy, muscular ass when he crossed the room, heading for an open doorway located in the corner. His butt cheeks flexed with every step. "Okay."

He paused at the doorway to look back at her. "Just don't attempt to leave the apartment. Please, Charlie."

Her body tensed. "I'm a prisoner?"

"This is your home," he corrected. "Remember how you did not enjoy being stared at while we were on the street? I won't be with you. I'm afraid someone would stop you to discover whom you belong to. No one will hurt you on Garden but you wouldn't enjoy being detained until I arrived to collect you."

"They'd lock me up?"

He ran his fingers through his dark hair. "I do not believe so but they wouldn't be comfortable allowing an unescorted human to walk the streets. The odds are, you would be halted, kept in place until I could be notified, and then I would have to come escort you home. I want your word of honor to never attempt to leave the city walls. I'm familiar with your skills at hacking security measures."

"What is outside the city?"

"Danger. We're not the sole inhabitants on this planet. They are not logical creatures, more amphibian than humanoid, and we have no idea what they would do if they ever captured someone from the city. It's never happened before."

Curious, she sat up on the bed and crossed her legs, comfortable with her nakedness in front of Zorus. "What do they look like? I've seen a few aliens but only on vids. I never left Earth before I traveled with you."

"When I return home I will show you. We have vids of them we study to learn more about their culture. We do not wish to interfere with their evolution. It is why we built a self-contained city to limit their contact with us." He paused. "I must get ready or I will be late. That would not be acceptable."

She waved her hand. "Go. I'm a big girl. I can amuse myself."

He flashed a grin. "You may borrow my clothing. I will have someone come measure you to have a wardrobe created for you tomorrow."

"Do I get to wear the stuff you do that looks like leather?"

"Do you wish to?"

"I'd like a few outfits made from it."

"Then I'll order you some." He walked out of sight then into the bathroom, but left the door open.

Charlie climbed off the big bed when she heard water come on in the next room. She investigated his closets and dresser drawers until she found a large, soft, cotton button-down-collar shirt to wear. The hem fell to her thighs. She borrowed a pair of his soft boxers but had to roll the waist to fit her better. She then left the bedroom to explore the apartment.

Zorus found her exploring his kitchen pantry. He brushed a kiss onto her upturned face. "I will not be gone long. They called this meeting to find out what happened to me while I was detained on Earth. I also need to be updated on what has happened while I've been away. I shouldn't be gone longer than an hour. The council building is very close."

"I'll be here." She smiled.

"Do you promise not to leave?"

He looked so solemn that she had to bite back a laugh. "I promise I won't go anywhere. Hurry back. I'll try to make us dinner with what you have in your kitchen but I admit, I'm not sure what some of this stuff is. I'm not a bad cook though and can probably whip up something good."

Charlie watched him go, missing him already, but then turned back to his food supplies. The guy had an abundance of everything. She'd gone from living in a crappy apartment to having the best the cyborg world could offer.

* * * * *

Zorus pushed his anger down. Two of the male council members who shared a human female in their family unit had purposely angered him with their petty smirks and comments over him bringing a human to Garden with him. He just wanted to leave the council building but a female cyborg had demanded to speak to him first. He sat behind his desk, his attention on the female who sat in a seat opposite him with the desk between them. He'd led her into his private office after the council meeting ended She had insisted on privacy.

"What is it, Alis?"

The tall female appeared irritated. "I want access to Sky. I have been informed that you sent him on a mission."

"For what purpose? He's my Earth expert."

"I wish to have a child. I want access to Sky for his sperm."

140

Zorus frowned. "He isn't part of a breeding pact any longer. The council purposely excluded him from one in consideration of his importance and the nature of his recent tasks he's been assigned to. Find a male who is on the list of males in your pact if you wish to have a child. That is what they were formed for. If the males of your family unit aren't able to conceive a child there are males with the pact who have viable sperm. They can assist you."

"I want Sky." Her voice lowered. "Before the council assigned him to his current position he used to be a member of my breeding pact. The first child I birthed is a result of his donation of sperm."

Frustration had Zorus tapping his fingers on the desk. He wanted to get home to Charlie. "What is your point?"

"I wish to have another who resembles my oldest son."

"I've assigned him off Garden. He's currently on his way to his new listening station. He's our Earth expert and therefore best to serve that job."

"I heard you were angry with him for some reason." The female stood and reached for her uniform. "I will bargain with you. You may have use of my body for the availability of his sperm."

When the female started to loosen her clothing, it brought Zorus to his feet. "No."

She paused, her uniform shirt open down the front. "It's an acceptable trade. You are a council member without a female and have basic needs. You've always bargained your favors in the past with intercourse."

"Not anymore."

Surprise widened her green eyes. "I am a healthy, attractive female. I cleared it with the males of my family unit before I came here. They are aware that I am prepared make this exchange."

"No," Zorus repeated, an image of Charlie fixed inside his mind. She wouldn't approve if he touched another female. She'd refused to take the human Gerald back after he left her for another female. "I no longer exchange favors for intercourse. I have a female of my own now."

"You are not joined in a family unit. I would have heard if you had." She frowned. "I really want access to Sky."

He stormed to the door. "No. Find another male if you wish to have a child. Sky will not be returning to Garden in the near future." Anger still burned inside him at Sky's interference with Charlie by making her fear he'd fooled her into a false sense of trust. "He is on an important mission." *Far from Garden and unable to cause more trouble with Charlie*, he added silently. "I haven't joined a family unit yet with my female but I plan to." He slammed out of his office.

He refused to do anything to risk Charlie's total agreement to remain with him. Not only that, he had to admit that the thought of touching another female left him cold and uninterested. It seemed as if it would be a chore, something unpleasant, if he had to have intercourse with anyone except Charlie.

He smiled faintly. Charlie was unique and wonderful. She stirred him in all ways, the only female he longed to touch, and he made a mental note to circulate the fact that he no longer traded favors to females for intercourse.

Chapter Nine

Charlie walked out of the bedroom feeling refreshed. The water on Garden was a lot cleaner, in her opinion, than what she bathed in on Earth. She'd brushed out her damp hair until all the tangles were gone. She'd have to ask Zorus where he hid his hair dryer. She hoped he'd return soon. Dinner would be ready to pull out of the oven in twenty minutes.

The sound of the elevator opening made her grin. She nearly ran down the hallway into the large living space. She came to an abrupt halt when a tall cyborg stalked into the center of the room. He froze when his dark gaze met hers.

He wasn't as tall as his father, but the strong resemblance left no doubt who she stared at. A frown creased his features, making him appear even more similar to Zorus.

"Hello." She shifted her stance, reached for the hem of the borrowed shirt to tug it down her thighs as much as she could, more than a little aware how much of her legs were exposed. "Your father isn't here. He had a council meeting to attend." Her mind drew a blank on the guy's name. She couldn't remember Zorus ever telling her that information. "I'm sure he'll be here soon."

"Human." He snarled the word.

Charlie took a step back. "I'm Charlie."

"What are you doing here?" His hands fisted at his sides.

"I live with your father." *Talk about uncomfortable.* "I'm sure he would have told you but we just arrived about two hours ago."

His dark eyes exactly like Zorus' narrowed dangerously. "He brought you with him from Earth?"

"Yes." She swallowed. "Please take a seat while I go put on some pants. I apologize. I didn't know you were coming to visit."

He stood there, silent, and continued to glare at her. She spun on her heel, embarrassed at her half-undressed state, and silently promised to have a little talk with Zorus when he returned. He should have warned her that his son had a tendency to drop by unannounced and had access to the apartment. If she'd known, she wouldn't have walked around in just a shirt and a pair of boxers.

Charlie entered the bedroom quickly and closed the door. She softly cursed before heading for the dresser. She'd seen some soft cotton-like breeches in a lower drawer when she'd explored earlier. She doubted they'd fit well but she'd rather wear loose pants than none at all around a stranger. She had reached the dresser when the door opened behind her. It hit the wall hard. The loud sound made her spin in surprise.

The cyborg glared at her, his gaze fixed on her, and rage his features. "What did you do to my father on Earth?"

Charlie backed up until she bumped the dresser. "Nothing. I helped him escape."

The big cyborg stalked into the room, eating up the distance between them with his long legs, and grabbed her before she could recover from the shock of his rage, directed at her. Two big hands gripped her upper arms.

144

She gasped painfully when he threw her. She cried out as her body flew through the air and then landed with a bounce on the massive bed.

"My father hates humans." He yelled the words.

Charlie pushed up from where she lay sprawled on her side where she'd landed, her terrified gaze locked with his. "He doesn't hate me," she got out before he grabbed her ankle.

"What did you do to my father?" He bent over her, dragged her to the side of the bed by her leg, and clamped one hand around her throat. He leaned over her body, snarled, and his hand tightened enough to cut off her air. "Did you abuse him? That's what you animals do."

Shock and terror held her immobile for seconds until she realized she couldn't breathe. Her hands clawed at his on her throat while she shook her head at him. He had it all wrong and he wouldn't even allow her to talk.

"My father told me what you humans did to him in the past. If he brought you here it would only be to implement his revenge on you."

Charlie managed to get her foot against the cyborg's chest, kicked out hard, and broke his hold on her throat. She rolled away on the bed, gasping in air.

"That's not how it is," she choked out before he grabbed her again.

He roared in rage, his hand closing over the back of her calf. Pain caused Charlie to scream when his fingers dug into the muscle on the back of her leg. She flipped over to kick out at him with her free leg. She slammed her foot into his face.

The guy reeled back, released her, but he staggered back. Red blood dripped from his nose where she'd nailed him but the enraged look in his eyes assured her that she may have just signed her own death warrant.

She rolled again to put more distance between them until the headboard halted her. "Zorus doesn't want me hurt. I swear I'm not the enemy. I'm his girlfriend. He—"

"Has fooled you," the man roared. He lifted a leg, one large boot stepped onto the end of the bed, and then he stood on it. "I won't kill you but I'll start teaching you the price of being human before he returns. I don't want to disappoint him from getting his personal revenge by killing you himself."

"He doesn't want me hurt!" Pure terror jolted through her.

She tried to avoid his hands when he bent and lunged at her but he grabbed her hair. Another scream tore from her throat. He jerked her hard, yanked her up with the handful of hair he gripped, and then stepped off the bed. He dragged her to the edge and she fell off. Agony shot throughout her body when she slammed hard into the floor and tears blinded her from the pain. She couldn't even breathe through the intense hurt, to scream again.

His hand grabbed the back of her shirt, jerked hard enough to lift her from the floor, and he just ripped it from her body. He shoved hard, slamming her face into the soft mattress, and her knees collapsed against the carpet. She took ragged breaths but was still in too much pain to even whimper. The sound of ripping material barely registered in her mind. She was too filled with shock and pain to understand what she heard.

Something brushed her face as he yanked her head back and a thick wad of material pushed against her mouth. He pulled her hair, causing more pain, and then she realized what he'd done. He'd stuffed a gag in her mouth and tied a thick strip of fabric around her head to keep it there, just under her nose. She screamed against the gag he'd made with part of the shirt but the sound came out muffled. Bruising hands gripped her arms to lift her limp body. He dumped her onto the bed facedown.

Stunned, reeling from pain, Charlie couldn't pull it together enough to fight when his hands slid down her arms to her wrists, which he wrenched behind her back. He used another torn strip to bind her hands together, tight enough to hurt. He gripped her shoulders, forced her to stand on trembling legs, and shoved her forward. She blinked back fresh tears that blinded her, just in time to see the dresser loom in front of her. Her hip hit the edge of it hard. She cried out against the gag.

Zorus! She screamed his name inside her mind but knew he couldn't hear her. His son pinned her on her feet against the dresser. His big body kept her hips shoved against the edge of the unforgiving wood furniture, and he released her shoulders. One hand grabbed the back of her neck and pushed her forward until her face touched the wall.

"My father told me what you animals did to him while he remained a prisoner inside the labs on Earth." His hips shifted to the side, still pinning her painfully, and the cyborg leaned over to snarl in her ear as he tore the boxers from her body. "Is that what you did to him when you had him this time? Did you chain him up, drug him, and abuse his body?"

She frantically shook her head, tried to deny it around the gag, but the sobbed words weren't even something she could understand. He couldn't possibly understand her protests.

"How does it feel to be naked and helpless?" Rage laced his voice.

Charlie sobbed. Her head hurt where he'd pulled her hair. She was sure he'd torn out some. Her calf, where he'd grabbed it, throbbed, bruised for sure, and his hip dug into her where he had her painfully pinned. She wanted to scream from the agony coursing throughout her body.

"The women were bad enough, strapping him down to use for their pleasure. They forced drugs into his system and shut off his implants to make him lose control of his own body, but the males were worse. Two of the male guards raped him often as punishment when he wouldn't comply."

Charlie turned cold inside at hearing that news, horrified. Zorus hadn't told her that. She understood why he'd hate humans, after all he'd endured, but that made it so much worse. He was a proud man. Being the victim of sexual assault would have been horrible enough but by men too?

"He told me of the pain. They would strap him down and force him to endure their animal lust. They taunted him, laughed when they made him bleed, and shamed him by calling him nothing but a toy to play with."

A hand grabbed Charlie's ass. "Have you ever taken a male here?" His fingers pressed against her anus. "I am told it hurts. They didn't care if he screamed. They didn't care if he bled. They enjoyed his suffering."

He jerked his hand away. Charlie screamed when she heard the sound of his pants being opened.

"You're going to know his pain."

Charlie tried to fight, tried to get away from him, but he kept her immobile against the dresser with his hand still gripping the back of her neck. His hot breath fanned her throat, another snarl coming from him.

"I'm going to enjoy every painful moment you suffer," he swore. "You're nothing but a toy for me to play with now."

* * * * *

Zorus smiled when he entered his apartment. The smell of the meal Charlie had prepared greeted him when the elevator doors opened. His gaze swept the kitchen and living area, searching for her as he strode inside. His stomach rumbled from hunger and the tempting scents of something he couldn't identify but wanted to eat.

"Charlie?" He headed for the bedroom when he didn't see her.

He froze at the open doorway at the sight of Darius. His son had his pants down to the back of his thighs to reveal his bare ass, faced the dresser, and as their gazes met, he saw blood dripping from his nose down his face. A muffled scream made his heart nearly stop before rage engulfed him. He moved before he even understood why his son had ventured inside his bedroom half undressed.

Darius turned more and in that instant Zorus saw what his son's body had shielded him from. Darius had Charlie wedged against the dresser, bent over it, her hands tied behind her back, and a red mark the size of a fist showed on her bare body, on her ass. He heard the anguished sound of horrified shock that came from his own lips.

149

Zorus lunged, roaring in rage, and before he knew it, he'd grabbed his son and thrown him away from Charlie. Her body shook and her muffled sobs tore at his gut. That's when he realized something was tied around her head. She'd slumped against the dresser the instant he'd thrown Darius away from her but he managed to catch her within his arms before she slid to the floor.

"What did you do?" Zorus roared, his head jerking to glare at his son, while he clutched Charlie's shaking body inside the cradle of his arms.

Darius lay sprawled on the floor where he'd landed roughly on his side. It only took Zorus a second to see the state of his son's aroused body to guess what he'd interrupted. He roared out in rage again, watched his son pale and his dark eyes widen with alarm.

Charlie sobbed, her body trembled hard against his, and the muffled noise dragged his infuriated focus to her. He turned her gently in his hold to get a look at her face. Tears streamed from her eyes, hair stuck to her face from the wetness, and a wide strip of torn clothing hid her mouth. Zorus sank to the floor, his legs giving out on him, but managed to cushion her when he fell. The look in Charlie's eyes tore him apart inside. Her fear and pain was so strong that he could almost feel them himself.

Zorus couldn't get breath into his lungs. His mind tried to function but the awfulness of the situation made thinking hard to do. He eased Charlie closer on his lap. His hands trembled badly as he tried to free her from the gag. He knew he pulled her hair but couldn't avoid it. The material had been tied with strands of it tangled into the knot. The second he gently removed it from her mouth, Charlie screamed.

The ragged, gut-wrenching sound tore through the room, pierced not only his ears with her pain but his heart. She sucked in air and threw her face against his chest. Great sobs racked her body. His arms wrapped around her only to realize her hands were still bound behind her back. He reached for them.

"Father?"

Zorus turned his head, fury finally burning through his distress. Darius had sat up and jerked his pants back into place on his hips but he hadn't fastened them. Zorus' fingers worked the knots that bound Charlie's wrists until he freed her. Her hands clutched at his shirt while she sobbed against him.

"I'm sorry if I should have waited to start torturing her."

It took everything for Zorus to get words out of his mouth. He wanted to scream the way Charlie had. "Did you rape her?"

"I was just about to."

Zorus felt a coldness settle into his soul while he glared at his son. "Did you enter her?"

"I was working on that when you walked in. She's very small and wouldn't easily take me." Darius slowly climbed to his feet. He scowled down at his father and then the woman on his lap. "What are you doing, freeing her?"

Zorus attempted to move Charlie off his lap to deal with his son but she cried out, clung to him tighter, and made it impossible for him to ease her onto the floor next to him. He froze. Emotions nearly overwhelmed him while they tore him in half. His son had attacked the woman he loved.

Darius had tried to rape Charlie, had assaulted her, and he wanted to beat on his own flesh and blood so badly that he quaked from the force of desire to kill the son he loved. He closed his eyes.

"Go," he rasped. "Leave, Darius."

"Father? What is wrong? Did I ruin your plans for her? Were you still playing the nice game with her?"

Zorus glowered at his son. "You attacked her." He paused—had to when his voice broke. "I don't want to kill you. I'm that angry at this moment. You had no authority to touch Charlie." His voice rose until he yelled. "She means something to me. Do you know what you've done? Do you understand I'd like nothing better than to make you bleed? Pound on you until you no longer live? Leave!" He shouted the last word.

Darius gaped at him.

Zorus embraced Charlie's shaking, small form, trying to comfort them both, but knew it wasn't possible. He closed his eyes to fight the wrath that threatened to make him take the life of his only son.

Long minutes passed before Charlie's sobs started to subside. Zorus opened his eyes to realize Darius no longer remained inside the room. He turned his head to make certain his son had left. He and Charlie were alone once again. He forced his numb body to move, to carefully cradle the woman he loved within his arms, and managed to get to his knees, then to his unsteady feet. He slowly walked into the bathroom.

Charlie got control of her emotions when Zorus eased her bare bottom onto the cool countertop and opened her eyes when he pulled away. She

152

didn't look at his face. She couldn't. Her body trembled, ached in too many places to count, but Zorus had arrived home in time to stop his son from raping her. She fought another sob that threatened at the memory of Darius pressing against her ass, trying to force his cock inside her.

"Charlie?" Zorus whispered her name. "I'm so sorry. Where do you hurt? What did he do to you?"

She wrapped her arms around her bare chest, hugged her body tightly, and kept her head down. More tears threatened to spill. She didn't know what to say to Zorus. She'd heard what he'd said to his son, the threat he'd made to kill him, and how upset he'd sounded.

"Charlie?" Zorus placed his hands gently on the tops of her thighs. She flinched, not meaning to, and inwardly winced when he jerked away. "I'm sorry."

"You didn't do this," she whispered.

An uncomfortable silence stretched. "Didn't I? I raised him to hate humans—all of them—and should have immediately spoken to him when I brought you into my home. I just didn't think of him. I had been told he'd returned to Garden after I was taken to Earth and I should have contacted him to warn him that I planned to live with you. I needed to make it clear what you mean to me, that you aren't the enemy. I should have ordered him to stay away from you if he couldn't accept you as an important part of my life."

She finally lifted her head to study Zorus. His handsome face looked ravaged with anguish, regret, and sadness. Hot tears blinded her until she blinked them back. "I'm going to be okay."

153

A muscle near his jaw twitched. "What did he do?"

She lowered her gaze. "I'm going to have some bruises and I may have some bald spots on the back of my head."

Zorus leaned closer until his body gently brushed against her knees while he examined the back of her head. "I don't see any."

"It feels like it. He pulled me around by my hair."

A soft growl came from him that made Charlie jerk her head up to stare at him. Anger darkened his features.

"I'm sorry."

"You didn't do it."

He opened his mouth.

"I know," she whispered before he could repeat taking the blame. "You feel responsible. Let's not go there, okay? I'm trying really hard to keep it together. I was terrified," she admitted. "If you hadn't walked in when—" Emotion choked her.

"He would have raped you."

She looked away from the rage burning in his dark gaze. "He tried."

Zorus moved closer to her again. "Let me wash you. It helps. You'll feel better once you clean away his touch."

She glanced up at Zorus, remembering what Darius had told her about his past. She didn't tell him what had been said but she had the sad insight that he knew from experience that bathing would help. No one had saved him from the humans who'd attacked him, raped and tortured him. She'd been spared the fate of being sexually abused.

Gentle hands helped her ease off the counter. She stood on trembling legs while he turned on the water inside the large tub located in one corner of the bathroom. She had longingly looked at it when she'd showered but hadn't wanted Zorus to return home to find her being lazy inside his bath.

"Dinner! There's a roast in the oven. It's going to burn."

"I'll remove it." He hesitated. "I'll return quickly."

She waited for him to leave before she faced a mirror. Red marks marred her skin on her upper arms, wrists, and shoulders. Her face looked red and her lips swollen from the gag that Darius had used. She turned then, lifted on tiptoe, and looked over her shoulder to get a view at her ass.

A red, angry mark showed on her ass cheek from where Darius had forced his hipbone against her there. A shiver ran up her spine at how close she'd been to being raped. A few more seconds and he would have entered her.

Zorus returned as quickly as he'd promised, stepped into the bathroom, and tested the temperature of the bath water. He turned and slowly started to undress. Charlie tensed.

"I'm not exactly in the mood now."

That drew an irritated look from him. "I don't wish to have sex. I want to go into the water with you, hold you, and wash you. Afterward I'll feed you dinner while you rest." He paused. "I just want to hold you. I need to. I could have lost you and I just—" His voice broke. "I want to hold you."

Hot tears blinded her but she blinked them back. "I'd like that."

He closed the distance between them in just his pants and boots, his strong arms pulling her against his chest in a tight hug, and she wrapped her arms around him.

"This will never happen again. I swear it to you, Charlie."

She nodded against his hot, bare chest. His body heat soothed her, warmed the cold places inside her that the attack had created, and she did feel safe.

"I will deal with my son." His tone turned icy.

Charlie suddenly shivered again. She didn't think Darius would enjoy whatever Zorus would say or do to his son. Not that she cared. Darius had shown no mercy for her and she wouldn't be broken up if he got his ass kicked by his father. Her only regret would be not watching as Zorus beat on him.

Chapter Ten

Zorus waited impatiently at the door to the apartment, three buildings from his own. He'd tried to calm the rage inside him. It had been difficult. He'd washed Charlie, cared for her, and she'd slept after he fed her the delicious meal she'd prepared.

Darius opened the door with a grim expression on his features. "Father."

"Son."

"You're angry."

"Furious."

Darius cocked his head and backed up. "Enter."

The apartment had a female's touch to the décor. Zorus glanced around. "Are your female and children of your family unit home?"

"This is her week to live with Urgo."

The thought of sending Charlie to live with another male made Zorus clench his fists. His son shared the woman of his family unit with two other males and whichever breeding-pact males were needed to conceive children if they needed outside help. He turned to face Darius when the door closed behind him.

"You had no authority to touch my female." His voice deepened. "Your female would be very angry if she knew you tried to have intercourse with another female."

Darius hesitated. "Not with a human. They are nothing but slaves for our use. My female understands that I have needs she isn't always around to fill."

"You are never," Zorus ground out each word, "to attempt to harm Charlie again. I don't even want you near her."

"She's just a human."

"She's mine!" Zorus snarled the words. He stepped back after he realized that he'd lunged forward a step when Darius backed up. He fought his fury, gained control of his emotions, and nearly flinched at the astounded expression on the face that so resembled his own.

"You care what happens to it?"

"Her. Charlie isn't my enemy, nor is she yours. Do you understand me? I plan to form a family unit with her."

Astonishment quickly transformed into anger on his son's face. Darius glared at his father. "She's somehow influenced you. You always said they could corrupt our people if given the opportunity. She has fooled you into believing she will not cause harm to you or our people. What did she do to you while you were a prisoner on Earth? Drug you? Torture you?"

"No. She rescued me and makes me happy."

Darius just gaped at him.

"I never believed I could care for a human either." Zorus paused to construct his thoughts into words that would allow his son to understand. "She was a grunt on Earth, irrelevant to Earth Government. Do you understand? She is similar to us in the way she has been treated by them all of her life. She has as much value to humans as we have on Earth. She's part of their disposable workforce. She risked her life to save mine numerous times."

"It's a trick you fell for." Darius spat the words contemptuously. "You have been deceived by the human. I understand the physical appeal. It must bring you much pleasure to have her under your control. I enjoyed her terror and the feel of her soft flesh. Give her to me and I'll kill her for you after I'm done using her."

Zorus would never have believed that he'd actually hit his son but that's exactly what he did in a blinding moment of rage. He watched as his son hit the carpet on his ass, his fist throbbed from the impact it had made with Darius' face. Zorus cursed under his breath.

"Don't ever touch her again. I realize this is my fault. I conditioned you to hate all humans but Charlie is different. You had better never speak of her in that regard again."

Blood trickled down Darius' chin from his busted lip. He defiantly stared up at his father. "You hate humans."

"I hate most humans but not Charlie."

"They abused you. Humans did horrendous things to you when they held you prisoner on Earth."

"You are correct." Zorus paused. "She didn't harm me in any way. She doesn't deserve your disgust or your need to seek vengeance on my behalf for what other humans once did to me."

"They are animals."

"Most of them are but not Charlie."

"You've been deceived. She will kill you while you sleep or she is a spy Earth Government sent to obtain information to exterminate us." Darius slowly rose to his feet, wiped away the blood from his lower face, and nodded at his father. "I will prove it to you. I'll make her confess the truth if you only allow me to interrogate her."

"You will not go anywhere near Charlie ever again. I have changed the codes that gave you access to my home. You are no longer welcome there. If you wish to see me, I will come here or we shall meet somewhere we both agree on." Zorus watched his son, his body tense. "You will never touch her again, son. I will do anything to defend her, even if that means protecting her from you."

Darius was clearly outraged. "You—"

"I mean it." Zorus hoped his son saw the sincerity in his serious gaze. His chest hurt over the fact that he'd had to take this strong position but he'd never allow anyone to hurt the woman he'd come to love. Not even his only son. "You go near her and I will consider you a threat to her life. I will defend her against an attack. I plan to form a family unit with her. Have I made myself clear on this matter? I didn't come here to debate the issue with you but to inform you of the serious nature of my relationship ties to the human."

Darius straightened to his full height, his body tensing. "I'm going to call a council meeting immediately. You have been compromised, your logic is no longer sound, and you are a traitor to all cyborgs if you choose a human over your own son."

Sadness crept inside Zorus to the point that he actually had to blink back tears. "You've never loved a woman, have you? You've never experienced true emotion or allowed anyone to mean so much to you that you will do anything to protect them."

"I had those emotions for my father but he must have died when he was taken to Earth." Disgust twisted his son's features. "Get out of my home. I will not stop until you are stripped of your position and your human is killed. I will save you from whatever she has done to you."

Zorus would not argue with someone who obviously refused to hear reason. He strode out of the apartment and tried to get control of his emotions. Ever since Charlie had come into his life it had spiraled out of control. He didn't regret it though. For once in his life he had something to live for. Charlie gave him contentment.

When he returned home, he placed calls to a few of the supportive council members who had either taken a human into their family units or backed the right to be with one. He hated to admit that his own son planned to bring charges against him but he knew Darius wouldn't make empty threats. When he finished the last notification, he walked quietly into the bedroom. Charlie had left the bathroom light on to keep the bedroom from total darkness.

She hugged his pillow, her body curled into a fetal position on her side in the middle of his bed, and his anger abated over the embarrassing situation his son had forced him to deal with. He quickly stripped and climbed onto the bed with Charlie. The moment he touched her, she jerked awake, gasped, and her terrified gaze flashed to his.

161

"It's just me, Charlie. I'm home. You're safe." He inched closer to her under the covers and rolled onto his back. He hated the fear she now had to deal with over what his son had done to her. "I didn't mean to startle you."

She curled toward his side, pressed her body tightly against his, and a protective urge gripped him so strongly it made breathing difficult. His arms encircled her to hold her closer to him.

"Are you okay? I know you went to see Darius. I woke and you were gone."

Her concern made him feel even more certain that he'd made the correct decision. "It did not go as I'd hoped. He doesn't agree with my choice to be with you. He refuses to accept my feelings and isn't capable of understanding why I am so protective of you."

She lifted her chin to gaze up at him, sadness reflected in her beautiful eyes. He also saw tears fill them and one slid down her cheek. He shifted his hold to gently brush it away with his thumb.

"Don't cry. No one will ever harm you again. I'm taking some time away from the council to stay at home for a while. I won't leave you alone to give him a second opportunity to harm you. Don't be afraid, Charlie."

"It's not that." She sniffed. "I'm so sorry that I'm the reason you and your son are fighting. He's an asshole for what he did to me but he's still your kid. I know you have to be really messed up over this. Are you okay? I know how it hurts when family does something totally screwed up. Remember my brother? He always could hurt me the most when he did stupid things."

"He sold you." A new sense of understanding of family betrayal became clear to Zorus in that moment. "How do you deal with loving someone who goes against you?"

"Eventually they hurt you enough that you stop allowing them to do it. At least you tell yourself that until the next time they do something else you never thought they were capable of." Charlie snuggled more firmly against him and rested her cheek on his chest. "It still hurts but you can't control the people you love. You just try to harden your heart as much as you can."

Zorus lifted his gaze to study the bedroom ceiling. "Will you hurt me, Charlie?"

She shook her head. "No. I know how it feels to open yourself up to someone and have them tear you apart. I'd never do that to you. I can just hope you won't ever do that to me either."

"I fear you will hurt me in some way. Emotions are new to me yet I've allowed you to matter too much in such a short time. But I would never intentionally hurt you."

"Welcome to my world," she suddenly chuckled. "Falling in love is never easy but here we are."

He tensed and looked down at the top of her head. Charlie tilted her face to gaze at him.

"What? You think I'd agree to come to your planet, leave everything behind, just because the sex is awesome?" She smiled.

"Say it."

"I love you, Zorus."

He couldn't stop the grin that curved his lips or the sheer joy that filled him to the point that he wasn't sure he could survive it.

"This is where you're supposed to either say it back or roll away."

"I attacked and threatened my own son to defend you. I made it clear I would kill him if he ever touches you again."

Charlie lifted up a little and rested her chin on the back of her hands on his chest. "Say it, Zorus. Please? I want to hear the words from you. I know you probably won't understand this but it means a lot to me."

"I love you, Charlie."

"That wasn't so hard, was it? Thank you."

"No but a part of me is definitely hard now."

She turned her head and grinned down his body where she couldn't miss the tented covers. She met his gaze again. "I see."

"I won't act upon it. I realize you are still traumatized."

That killed her happy mood. "Yeah."

"Time will help you get past this."

She didn't miss the haunted tone of his voice. "You know that for sure, don't you?"

His body under hers stiffened but then relaxed again. "Yes."

"Do you want to talk about it?"

He drew in a ragged breath. "I told you about some of the abuse I suffered. They didn't consider me a living being. They believed me to be a thing without thought or feeling. I had both." He took a few more breaths. "I know my son attacked you in some misguided sense of vengeance for what I suffered back in the days when Earth Government controlled us. I never told him of what I endured but he saw the reports about nine years ago. We all had to file reports on our experiences while in captivity. He's a doctor and has access to them. He read every page of my reports."

"Did you ever talk to him about it?"

He nodded. "He came to me immediately and we discussed it at length. I taught him to hate humans before he knew exactly what had been done to me but it became worse after he read the accounts. When the bounty hunters were captured, he helped me lure them into a sense of friendship to get them to be truthful. He also helped me kill them."

Charlie pressed tighter to Zorus to feel his warmth when a chill crept up her spine. "You enjoyed killing them, didn't you?"

"They weren't the types of humans who were decent."

She remembered some of the guys she'd grown up with. A good percentage of them had grown up to be rapists, murderers, or thugs. Some fell into all three of those categories. The idea of them dying didn't choke her up in the least. "I know some humans are evil."

"They wanted to destroy us. It's my job to protect my people."

"Those scientists planned to autopsy you."

"They think nothing of our right to life. We are things to them. Experiments or objects to use for whatever purpose they desire."

She nodded against his chest. "I get it. I'm not the enemy though."

"I know that. You are unique."

"Not all humans are bad."

"To me you are the exception to the rule."

She smiled. "I'm glad. I'd hate to be on your bad side."

"That could never happen, Charlie. I chose you over my son. This stuns me but it is the truth. I swore to always be honest with you. I won't allow him near you again. I would kill one of my own people to protect you from any harm. You matter to me that much. I may not easily say words of love but that is what I feel for you. I have never allowed emotions to control me yet I have had no wish to suppress them since we met. You are more than worth the risk of pain I face by trusting you."

"I'm glad."

"You agreed to come home with me. I do understand and acknowledge how difficult a decision that had to be for you to make. You've been very brave." He paused. "It is yet another trait about you I find appealing."

"Love is a crazy thing, isn't it? It hits when you least expect it, grabs you by the shorthairs, and tugs you in whatever direction it decides to go."

Zorus chuckled. "Your words amuse me."

Her hand slid down his chest, over his flat belly, and lower until her fingertips stopped at the base of his cock. He'd softened slightly but not by much. She wrapped her hand around him to stroke him under the covers. He tensed.

"What are you doing?"

"What does it feel like?"

"You don't need to alleviate my desire for sexual release. I don't expect it, Charlie. You have been through a trauma. I'm capable of controlling my body. I do not suffer as a human male would."

"And do you know what I think is the best way to heal?" She lifted her head to stare into his beautiful gaze. "Make love to me. Erase the bad memories with good ones. You kiss me and I can't think. You burn me up with your touch to take away the coldness."

He didn't argue with her. She feared he would but instead he slowly turned onto his side, used his body to ease her onto hers, and then slid down until she had to release her hold on his cock. He flattened his hand on her stomach to nudge her all the way onto her back. She smiled when he moved to his knees and put one between her legs. She spread her thighs wide apart to make more room for him.

"I know how to make you hot." His head dipped to brush a kiss on her hip.

Charlie smiled. "I love your mouth."

"I know."

She laughed at his smug comment. "You definitely are talented with it."

His hands tapped her thighs and she parted them more, lifted her knees a little, and gave him full access to her sex. He slid his palms under her ass to lift her closer to his parted lips. She gasped a little from a dull stab of pain when he did it but she bit her lip to refrain from mentioning the bruise there. He froze.

"Do you want to stop?"

"No."

He released her ass carefully. "I forgot. I'm sorry."

"Grip my hips."

He adjusted his body and got a new hold on her. She knew she wiggled a lot when he went down on her and he preferred to pin her immobile. She relaxed, waited, and then his tongue teased her clit. The hesitancy when he licked her saddened her. She knew he probably worried she'd become frightened.

"I know it's you," she whispered. "I love you. I want you, Zorus."

His lips enclosed her clit, the flat of his tongue rapidly moved back and forth, and Charlie moaned. Desire quickly ignited throughout her body. She reached up to grab the pillow just for something to hold onto.

"Yes," she moaned. "That is so good."

He groaned against her, the soft vibration driving her pleasure higher. She arched her back to press tighter against his hot mouth. His teeth lightly raked over the sensitive nerve endings and she realized how close she hovered near climax.

"Stop."

Zorus tore his mouth from her. "Did I hurt you?"

She really hated the worry she heard in his tone. "No. I want you inside me when I come."

He moved on the bed but instead of climbing over her, he sprawled out next to her body, and rolled flat onto his back.

"Ride me," he urged. "I want you to know you're in control."

He never ceased to amaze her. He didn't want her to feel pinned or trapped. Her body ached and throbbed from his sensual kisses. She climbed to her knees, threw a leg over his hips, and hovered there. She gripped his rock-hard cock with one hand and flattened her other one on his chest for leverage. She looked down between their bodies, her hair fell across him as she guided his cock to the opening of her pussy. He softly groaned her name when she slowly settled down on the thick shaft. The crown of it stretched her apart to accept more of him.

Sheer delight radiated from her core when she lowered on top of Zorus. Her inner nerve endings sizzled when he stretched her vaginal walls, filled the need she craved, and she threw her head back with a moan. She paused when she'd taken all of him. Her pussy clenched around him to draw a soft moan from both of them.

"You're so beautiful," Zorus rasped. "I love you, Charlie."

She met his gaze in the dim room, his eyes dark and sincere. "I love you too."

His hands lightly caressed her hips, urged her to move, and she lifted up and then slowly lowered. Pleasure rippled through her from the snug fit of their bodies joined together. Charlie started to move up and down, finding a pace that felt the best. Zorus was extremely hard, thick, and each motion brought her sheer delight. When the need to come became nearly overwhelming, she rode him hard and fast. The sound of their heavy breathing and the slap of her bottom on the top of his thighs turned her on even more.

Zorus slid his hand from his light grip around the curve of her hip to dip his fingers between her spread thighs. He sought and found her clit to press the side of his thumb there. With every slide of their bodies it brushed her swollen bud until it sent her over the edge. Rapture seized her.

Charlie threw her head back, cried out his name, and under her, Zorus snarled her name. She knew her vaginal walls were strongly convulsing around his cock, massaging him as he found his own release, and she loved feeling him filling her with his warm semen. She collapsed on top of him when she couldn't remain upright anymore.

His two strong arms hugged her tightly around her waist and he pressed a kiss to her sweaty forehead. A chuckle made him shake a little under her.

"What's funny?" She didn't lift her head to look at him, too spent to do more than lie sprawled on his chest. She loved hearing his heart beating erratically under her ear.

"I'm just happy, Charlie. You are the best thing that has ever happened to my life."

A smile curved her lips. "I've never been happier either."

Chapter Eleven

Zorus appeared nervous, which made Charlie feel the same. He'd taken a call early that morning, had been grim ever since, and now they had to go to a council meeting. He'd informed Charlie that she needed to attend with him.

"What is going on? You said you'd be honest with me but you keep avoiding my questions." It didn't help that the clothes she wore were his, hung on her body loosely, and he'd had to cut off the legs and arms to fit her shorter limbs. She knew she'd make a sad sight in public. "Does this have something to do with your son?"

He'd barely touched breakfast when his gaze lifted to meet hers over the table in the kitchen. "Yes. He's decided to file charges against me."

Her heart missed a beat. "What kind of charges? Criminal ones? He's the one who assaulted me inside your home. You were just protecting me when you threw him to the floor."

"He's accused me of treason."

The color drained from her face and she nearly dropped her fork. "On Earth that's a death sentence. How the hell could he do that? Why would he? What is the logic in doing that? I thought you said your society was based on logic."

"I feel certain he believes it's true because I chose you, a human, over my own son. He's angry."

Her appetite fled. "This council will know it's bullshit, right? You're all about your people. You've killed to protect them."

"I warned a few members this might happen." He focused his attention on his plate. "I don't want you to worry, Charlie. I'm nearly certain this will be resolved in my favor."

"Nearly certain?" Her hand trembled when she set her fork down carefully to avoid it clattering on the glass surface of the table. "What happens if they buy his bullshit? What if they think he's right? What is the punishment for treason here?"

"The same as if we were on Earth."

"They could kill you?" She shot to her feet. "Zorus…"

Cool, brown eyes fixed on her. "Sit and finish your meal. They won't execute me. I've been too loyal for far too many years for any member to believe I'm capable of disloyalty."

"I'm trying not to freak out but I've only met a few other cyborgs. They didn't like you at all. I'd even go so far as to say they flat out hated you. What if this council uses this charge as a way to get rid of you?" She spun to pace the floor, her mind reeling from what could happen. "We need to flee. Yeah. We'll steal a ship, get off the planet, and go to Saturn." She jerked to a halt to glance at him. "Or one of the stations. We need to get to Saturn first though. I'll get my money from Russell so we aren't broke. We'll need money to survive. We'll be okay as long as we're together. We'll make it work somehow."

Zorus stood. "Calm down. It will not go that far. My son is angry, the council members, for the most part, do not hate me. It may surprise you to

172

know that I do have some friends. It would take a unanimous vote to bring about my death."

Anguish gripped Charlie. "Did you know this might happen? Is being with me so horrible on this planet that someone could accuse you of being a traitor?"

He shrugged. "A cyborg hasn't taken a human yet when...shit hasn't hit the fan." His lips twitched. "I remember that Earth saying. I expected issues to arise. This wasn't a scenario I anticipated but it's actually less severe than some of the others that came to mind."

"What could be worse?" She chewed her lower lip.

"They could have attempted to take you from me to give to another male."

A shiver ran down her spine. "Is that possible?"

"No. I discarded that prospect. The law is on my side."

"What else?"

"They could ban me from the council but I know it's highly unlikely. Two members share a human in their family unit. I know they will avoid voting me out since it would weaken their own positions. They'll welcome a member with a human for that reason alone."

"They share?"

"I told you some females have more than one male." He sighed heavily. "You gave me your word you will never do that."

"And you never have to worry about me going back on it. You're more than enough for me." She relaxed slightly. "You're not worried?"

Zorus gave her a tense smile. "I am not worried of being found guilty of treason."

"Then why are you so grim?"

"It will be tense. Words will be spoken that I do not want you to hear." He took a few steps until he paused in front of her to gaze deeply at her. "I don't want you to stop loving me, Charlie. I never want to see fear or distrust in your eyes again." His hands brushed her arms, caressed her, and he took hold of both her hands. "You will hear things about me that will disturb you."

"Worse than the fact that you made friends with humans before you killed them by beating them to death or wanted other human women killed just for being with cyborg guys?"

"I have readily admitted that I was not fond of humans until I met you. They were my enemy, I am unforgiving of what has been done to me, and I've shown no mercy. You may hear examples of the things I've done to ensure the survival of my race as proof that my reasoning has been put into question by bringing you home with me. As a human, you may hate me for some of those examples."

Her stomach knotted. "Have you ever beaten a woman to death?"

He shook his head, a frown twisting his lips downward. "No."

"Raped one?"

"No!" Anger tinged his voice. "I would never do that to anyone."

"Killed a woman?"

Silence reigned. He didn't look away though. He took a few breaths before he spoke.

"I killed both male and females when we escaped Earth. They were guards, would have taken my life if I hadn't fired upon them first, and I have ordered the executions of a few female bounty hunters who have been transported to Garden."

"You made friends with the men." A horrible thought struck her. "Did you make friends with the women too?"

His hands tightened their hold. "Yes."

"You seduced them?"

His dark eyes narrowed. "I wouldn't word it in that manner."

"Had sex with them? Intercourse?"

He glanced away and then back. "Yes, Charlie. I had intercourse with two of them. I allowed them to believe the offer of use of their bodies worked, that I'd allow them to use me to gain freedom."

Her knees weakened but Zorus kept her up when he released her hands to grip her around her waist instead.

"I am not lying to you, Charlie. I do love you. I'd risk my own life to protect yours. This is what I feared. I can see the suspicion in your eyes right now. You're wondering if I've lied to you and how many humans I've deceived."

She couldn't deny it. Zorus softly swore, adjusted his hold on her, and swung her into his arms. She gasped but then curled into his lap when he dropped into a chair in the living room. He cupped her face to tilt her head until they studied each other.

"You never asked me to bring you to Garden. My son will accuse you of being an Earth spy. He already has made that allegation to me. I am willing to trust that you are not with me for that reason. You are a hacker yet you haven't touched my systems in an attempt to send a signal to Earth. The apartment is being monitored."

"You trust me but you still had me watched?"

"I took your skills into account, and had someone else take over monitoring my home last evening, but not because I don't trust you. It is a precaution in case my son accuses me of covering for you. You are similar to me, Charlie. Earth Government is your enemy. I know this but my son doesn't. By having a trusted third party monitor my home there is no doubt of your innocence. I'm not in a position to lie to protect you if you were guilty. I believe in you. I did it to prove both of us are innocent."

She glanced around the room. "What kind of monitoring? Are there cameras?"

He tugged on her chin to force her to look at him again. "There are no cameras or microphones present but if you attempt to breach the system in any way they will know. We have more advanced technology than Earth. I wouldn't have asked a friend to do it if I honestly believed you'd attempt to hack my system. A security team would arrive immediately to arrest you and all outgoing messages from Garden have to be approved first before they are broadcast to the satellites that carry the signals. There is no chance of you contacting anyone off the planet."

"I wouldn't do that."

"I know." Sincerity shone in his gaze. "I'd never have risked you being arrested if I had thought there was any chance you'd betray me."

She let his words sink in. It calmed her temper. If he were being accused of treason and she of being a spy, they both needed their butts covered. Zorus had done that to the best of his ability.

"What about those women?"

"There were two, as I stated. They were bounty hunters who wanted to collect the reward Earth has put out on cyborgs. They would have turned us over to Earth Government, knowing we would be killed. We have a few listening posts near some of the space stations that monitor traffic. We sent teams to collect anyone seeking information about our kind and bring them here to interrogate." His chest rose and fell. "Those females would have tried to either kill cyborgs with terrorist attacks or attempted to escape the planet to give Earth our location. The council unanimously agreed to their deaths to safeguard all cyborgs. I don't enjoy killing females but it fell to the council to decide their fates. I have no regrets for the choices we've made. Safeguarding my people is the council's priority. These humans, even the females, were a danger to all. They suffered no pain or fear. I do have some compassion."

"The men—"

"Died brutal deaths. If you believe they were tied down while beaten, you would be incorrect. They were given the choice of being painlessly executed or engaging in a fight to the death. They always chose violence. We did not give the females that option. Our female cyborgs are too valued to risk in a fight with another female and it wouldn't have been fair to make them fight against a male cyborg. They stood no chance at winning. It would have just been cruel."

Her attention lowered to the collar of his leather shirt. "Did you care for either of those women?"

"It was intercourse and a role to play. They weren't victims, Charlie. They were hardened females who decided they could use their bodies as a way to turn me on my own people to help them escape. They would have slit my throat the instant they were freed without hesitation once they no longer had use of me."

She lifted her gaze to study him closely. He honestly believed that. "Are you sure?"

"Yes, Charlie. I am certain. They had no real emotions for me."

She tucked her chin. "Okay."

"Look at me."

She met his beautiful eyes.

"I love you. I am not lying to you. This isn't a game or a charade to get information from you. Our relationship is based on trust and real emotions."

"I tend to believe you since I sure don't have anything you'd want." She gave him a sad smile. "I'm flat broke and all I have left are my boots and bra. You wouldn't fit into either of them."

"You do have something I want."

"What's that?"

"I want you, Charlie. Your sense of humor, your body, your touch, and the way you make me feel."

She had to blink back tears. "That's so sweet. Okay. I know we need to leave for this council meeting. Whatever they say, don't worry about me, okay? We're good. You told me the most important thing I need to know about you. The rest doesn't matter."

He hesitated again. "I pushed to make humans property."

"I knew that."

"If it hadn't been for my insistence, that law wouldn't have passed. I suffered great bitterness for all humans, had never known one such as you, and truly believed they held no compassion. I never saw any of them treat a cyborg as anything other than a thing. I wanted humans to learn what had been done to us firsthand. I wanted them to suffer, knowing they weren't counted as part of society but instead as just tools to be used as we wished."

"I get it." She wrapped her arm around his neck and used his shoulder to pillow her head in a way that she could continue to see his face. "I even understand how you'd feel that way."

"I also battled to have males share females. That may come up as well."

"Why?"

"Our population needed to increase. We were so few when we reached Garden, and the survival of our race depends on our ability to breed. A female with different lovers has a higher chance at procreation. My son knows that I also couldn't stand his mother. The idea of sending her to another male helped me argue for the breeding pact as it has been designed. I wasn't able to impregnate her with more children. I stated that I did it to make it possible for her to have other children." He sighed.

"You wanted her to be someone else's problem."

"Yes." He blushed just a little, his skin turning a dusky gray. "I didn't want to hurt her ego but the idea of passing her off to other males to live with made me argue with zest for that law."

"Any more secrets?"

He sighed. "None that I believe will make you dislike me enough to ask to live somewhere else."

"Okay. We're good."

"I appreciate that."

She eased her arm from around his neck, lifted up to plant a kiss on his cheek, and winked at him. "I'm not a saint either, hon. I just never had the ability to pass laws. I can think of some assholes I wouldn't have allowed to keep their nuts attached to their bodies. Ever heard that saying 'stupid people shouldn't breed'? Yeah. That would have been a law I'd have pushed hard to get passed." She climbed off his lap. "Let's get this over with."

Zorus stood and held out his hand to her. "My people will stare at us. No one will harm you."

"Too bad this time they have a reason to gawk." She glanced down her body. "I can't wait to have clothes that fit. Do I look as bad as I think I do? I feel as though I'm playing dress-up."

"You are…" He grinned. "Adorable."

"Right. My bullshit meter is over the line."

He laughed, tugged her toward the door, and she followed. Her chin lifted and she straightened her shoulders. She'd faced a lot of things in her life that she dreaded but this time she really didn't know what to expect. She trusted Zorus. He appeared relaxed now, unconcerned, and at ease.

The ride down the elevator seemed too short and then they left the building. Cyborgs paused to check Charlie out but none approached or said a word. Zorus kept her against his side, her hand held in his, and they reached a building she knew housed the council. Two large, mean-looking cyborgs blocked their way.

"Councilman Zorus." A blond one spoke. "We must check the human for weapons."

Irritation flashed but Zorus released her hand. "He will pat you down, Charlie. Spread your arms and legs please."

She did it but sent him a frown when the stranger crouched to run his big, gloved hands over her body. She blushed when he touched her in a few places but didn't protest. Zorus held out his hand the second the guard rose to his feet to back away.

"She's unarmed. They are waiting for you. Session has begun. The other members arrived early and your son is present."

"I didn't doubt he would show up."

The council room reminded her of a courtroom. Eleven seats were filled but one remained vacant behind the tall desk-like counter that formed a slightly curved table, like a judge's bench. She guessed that empty seat belonged to Zorus. Eight males and three females dressed in matching white shirts studied them silently.

Zorus led Charlie to two seats, like those used on Earth, usually designated for the defense. There weren't tables in this room set up for briefcases or papers. She sat on the chair, folded her hands in her lap to hide their trembling, and turned her head to watch more cyborgs quietly enter the room and fill the seats behind them. Obviously this would be a packed event.

"It will be fine," Zorus assured her softly under his breath, just loud enough for her to hear. "Remain quiet."

She nodded tensely. A side door opened, drawing her attention. Darius strode into the room with a dark-haired cyborg. Both men took seats where the prosecutors usually sat in Earth courtrooms. Approximately eight feet separated her from her attacker. She forced her gaze away to glance at anything but him.

The back doors closed along with the side door and guards stood in front of them. A woman on the council cleared her throat. "Begin."

A dark-haired cyborg spoke next. "We are the council of," a smirk twisted his lips, "twelve, minus one currently. I am Councilman Coval." The guy glanced at Darius but then gave his full attention to Zorus. "You've been accused of treason and your human female of being an Earth spy. What the hell is going on?"

"Coval," the woman next to him hissed. "This is an official council session. Refrain from your colorful usage of words."

"My apologies." He sighed. "I hate wasting time when I have better things to do. Address the charges, Zorus. Your title has been revoked during the proceedings. You stand accused of a very serious crime against Garden and all cyborgs. Your son, Darius, stated that you have been influenced by a human. Your loyalty has been brought into question."

Zorus shot an annoyed look at his son before he addressed the council. "This is a family matter that never should have been brought before the council. Darius entered my home last evening, attacked my human, and didn't agree with my intention to form a family unit with her in the future. I threatened him with bodily harm if he ever attempted to harm her again. He accused me of treason for protecting her."

By Charlie's count, at least six council members registered pure shock. Coval looked highly irritated as did the blond to his immediate right. One of the women on the council glowered at Darius. She leaned forward.

"Attacked? No mention was made of that before now. How did he attack your human, Zorus?"

Anger deepened his voice. "I walked into my bedroom to find he'd torn the clothing from her body, bruised her up, and he intended to rape her. He'd terrorized her, unprovoked. He'd bound her to prevent her from being able to fight him off."

Dark, dull gray wasn't a pretty color on the woman's features when she rose to her feet to almost bend over the table to grip the edge of it. Anger emanated from her when she focused on Darius.

"Is that true?"

Charlie slid a glance at Darius. His skin had paled a sickly ash gray.

183

"She's property. It's not as if she is a cyborg female."

The woman threw her body back hard enough to make the chair creak. Her green eyes glittered with rage. "I see you toed that line very carefully, didn't you?"

"Jazel," he croaked.

"Silence," she hissed while her hand jerked up, palm out. It then slammed flat into the table to make a loud noise. "We'll speak of this later, in private, after the meeting."

A soft chuckle escaped Zorus. Amusement glinted in his eyes when he met her gaze for an instant. He knew something she didn't but she could guess. Darius and the woman obviously knew each other since he'd called her by her first name, the fact that he'd tried to rape Charlie infuriated the woman, and Darius sported that "I'm in deep shit" look.

She leaned over enough to brush Zorus with her shoulder. "His wife?" she mouthed.

Zorus' grin widened. He stood instead of answering her and he wiped all emotion from his features. "The accusations are false. There isn't a question of my true loyalty to our people. I would ask the charges be dropped."

"She's a spy from Earth and has somehow twisted you inside," Darius ground out harshly. "I demand a physical examination be performed on my father to make sure he hasn't been drugged or tortured."

"She rescued me," Zorus stated coldly. "She planned to move to Saturn until I talked her in to coming here with me. She is not a spy from Earth." He glanced at each of the cyborg council. "She held the status of a grunt on Earth. She came from the working class, her classification almost the same ours. The government allowed the females of her family to die when the black flu hit. They gave her a male name to prevent her from being taken away to do as they saw fit when she survived her birth."

The dark-haired cyborg, Coval, leaned forward. "I am very interested in learning how a human became important to you."

The blond at his side grinned. "I am as well. Explain it in detail, Zorus. Humans are our enemy and not to be trusted. How did the female convince you otherwise?"

A deep growl came from Zorus. "You just want details, Rais." He crossed his arms over his chest. "Are you enjoying this?"

The blond chuckled. "Yes and you are on trial still. You must answer our questions."

A few of the council members chuckled. Charlie had a sinking sensation inside her gut that she was about to witness payback. A pale, blonde woman laughed aloud.

"Yes, Zorus. Do explain your sudden reversal on this matter. We have listened to years of your rants about how no human is trustworthy, they will ruin our society, and how dangerous they are." The woman pointed at Charlie. "No chains? She looks shifty."

"I do not," Charlie gasped before she could halt the words. Her mouth slammed closed.

Zorus gave her an irritated look before he faced the council. "You're enjoying this, aren't you? All of you?"

"Yes," a cyborg chuckled. "Explain it to us so we don't find you in contempt."

"Fine." Zorus dropped his hands to his sides, fisted them, and took a deep breath. "She makes me feel emotions. She makes me happy for once in my entire existence. I have discovered love." His words came out harshly, his anger clear. "So laugh if you will. I've fallen for the thing I hated most. I didn't mean for it to happen but she is unique. She risked her life countless times to save mine. She gave up her freedom for the belief that mine may have been in question. She once held a weapon on me," he turned his head again to meet Charlie's eyes. His features softened. "I noticed you adjusted the aim of it to make it impossible to kill me though you believed my intentions were deadly toward you." He faced the council again. "She's taught me not all humans are evil, intent on doing us harm, and made me finally understand what one of our males could see in a human female." He addressed Coval and Rais. "I apologize for every insult I've given to you both for choosing one of them over our own females."

Rais gawked. Coval nodded, his features suddenly serious. "Apology accepted on behalf of our family unit."

Jazel stood. "I've heard enough. Obviously the charges were greatly exaggerated by Darius." She glared at him. "Close your mouth and do not say another word. You have done enough damage today. I vote not guilty and this matter is closed. All in agreement?"

Every head nodded. Coval stood next. "All in agreement. Councilman Zorus, you have been cleared, your title reinstated, and this matter is dropped. There could never be a question of your integrity or loyalty to all of our people after your years of service with this council. We'll see you again when we meet next week." He paused. "Congratulations on finally embracing the things we fought so hard to establish the right to have. You are more than what Earth created you to be. You have stopped being cold inside, released the hatred you lived by, and have discovered the ability to love." He paused. "You are truly alive now."

Zorus hung his head, his body going unusually still, and the room started to clear. Charlie sat there watching the man she loved long after everyone left them alone. She had no idea what to say or do to help him with whatever thoughts were obviously weighing upon him so heavily.

Chapter Twelve

Zorus had been unusually silent on the walk home. Charlie kept glancing at him after they reached his apartment but he seemed to be on autopilot while he prepared food she doubted he'd touch.

"Are you all right?"

"I'm fine."

"No. You aren't. Ever since the council meeting, you look about as happy as a kid who just got a butt whipping. What is going on?"

He slowly turned. The look in his eyes seemed cold to her, distant, and his emotions were on lockdown, obviously.

"I did not predict the emotional ramifications of bringing you with me to Garden."

Her heart missed a beat while she tried not to show him the hurt that gripped her. "Are you sorry you brought me to Garden with you?" She hated to even ask. If he said yes it would not only break her heart but destroy the rest of her already fractured life.

"I am trying to adjust to the new circumstances."

"That's not an answer."

"My son distrusts me enough to publicly charge me with treason. The council always held great respect for my strong beliefs yet they just chastised me in an open meeting in front of my people." He drew in a deep breath. "They were amused by my humiliation. I never would have suffered that before I met you, Charlie. The emotional scales have been tipped. I am currently assessing how that affects me."

"Okay." She hid the tears that filled her eyes by turning on her heel. "You assess." She headed for the bedroom to put some distance between them.

Damn it, she thought when she stepped into his room. The view along the far wall remained breathtaking but it had lost all appeal to her. Zorus obviously regretted falling in love with her. She'd cost him a lot. He wasn't the only one who had lost but yelling at him for hurting her feelings when he'd already taken emotional hits today would only make matters worse.

I gave up my life too. Not that I really had one anymore after Russell got us into that jam. I've got the government looking for me, I'm a fugitive on the run from them, and I'm flat broke. I could have gone to Saturn to get my money. I could have started a life of my own but no. I decided to—

A loud buzz jerked her from her angry thoughts. She heard it again. It took her a moment to realize the source. She headed to the living room, hoping it wasn't someone else at the door who would give Zorus hell for being with a human. When she entered the large room, she paused at the shocking sight before her.

Zorus stood with his back to her while a woman dropped her coat onto the floor near the still-open elevator doors. Soft, metallic-gray skin had been revealed when the heavy leather landed on the floor. "I need Sky," the woman demanded. "You will have intercourse with me in exchange for the breeding right with him."

"What the hell?" Charlie's voice sounded too loud to her own ears but she was more than a little angry over the woman who demanded to fuck her boyfriend.

Zorus glanced at her over his shoulder. "This is nothing."

"I don't agree." She strode forward, her gaze fixed on the tall, beautiful, naked cyborg woman. "Who are you?"

The cyborg woman ignored Charlie. "I will not take no for an answer. We will exchange intercourse for your favor."

"Alis," Zorus growled. "I told you, Sky is on a mission. I also turned down your offer. I have not changed my mind." He glanced at Charlie again. "That is my human female. I told you that I plan to form a family unit with her."

The cyborg woman flicked her wrist in dismissal. "She's human. It isn't as though she could leave you. She's property." She stepped into Zorus, her body pressed flush to his, and she wrapped her arms around his neck to stare into his eyes. They nearly were eye level. "You know you will enjoy the physical connection we make. You always have in the past."

Charlie moved before she could think about what she'd do to the bigger, muscled, naked bitch who had just admitted she'd had Zorus in the past. Her jealousy at the sight of the other woman's arms around Zorus burned too hot to deny. She lunged but Zorus suddenly grabbed Alis around the waist to swing her out of the way. Charlie ended up with a handful of the back of his shirt rather than the woman's hair.

Zorus snarled at Charlie when he peered down at her over his shoulder. "Do not attack her, Charlie."

He might as well have slapped her. The pain hit her that sharply. She released his shirt, staggered back, and then tore her hurt-filled gaze away from his angry glare. She couldn't even talk. He released his hold on Alis with one arm only then reach up to tear her hands from behind his head.

Charlie couldn't stop the numbness that took over. She didn't know what to do or where to go. She darted toward the elevator, to leave. If he wanted to fuck the cyborg woman, she sure wasn't going to stick around. They were over. He regretted bringing her to Garden, obviously had decided to move on, but she wasn't about to watch him with his new girlfriend. She entered the lift but the doors didn't close. She reached for the controls. She'd hack it if she had to.

"Where are you going?" Zorus snarled the words. "Charlie? Get back in here."

She refused to look at him. The system wasn't one she'd ever seen. It didn't have a panel or any opening that she could detect. She tried voice command. "Down please."

The elevator doors didn't close. She gritted her teeth. "Bottom floor. Move, damn it. I want to leave."

"You're not going anywhere." Zorus stormed toward her.

From the corner of her eye, she saw him approach and jerked her head in his direction to give him a murderous glare. "Don't come near me. You made your choice. I bet your son will be thrilled that you've chosen a cyborg woman over me."

"Unreasonable females," he muttered a second before he gripped Charlie's arm in a firm hold to haul her out of the elevator.

She dug her heels in but he easily dragged her back into his living room. She yanked hard, attempting to break his hold on her. It didn't work.

"Do you see what you've done, Alis? Put your coat on and leave. I said no. I do not want to make an agreement with you." He gave Charlie's arm a rough tug. "I did not protect her for any of the reasons you must assume. She's a cyborg and you are human. If you draw blood from a cyborg on this planet, she can have you arrested."

Charlie ceased her struggles to peer up at him. He shook his head at her, an angry look plastered on his handsome features before he addressed Alis again.

"Get out and never return. Find another male to breed a child with. Sky will not be returning to Garden until his mission is complete. You have my word that you will never receive permission to spend another minute with him if you cause trouble for me again by pulling a stunt such as this one." He drew in a deep breath. "Leave."

Alis bent, showed off her muscular, smooth ass, and then pulled on her coat to conceal her nakedness. "You will regret this."

"I already do. I should have verified who wanted entry into my home. I wouldn't have permitted you onto my floor if I'd know you were there."

"You have lost your ability to be logical." She sneered at Charlie. "The human has impaired your intelligence."

"Get out." Zorus released Charlie to take a threatening step toward the cyborg. "She can't throw you into the elevator to get you out of our home but I can."

The threat hung in the air. Alis made tracks for the elevator. The moment she cleared the doors they slid closed. Zorus closed his eyes.

"I'm very angry."

"Me too," Charlie admitted.

His dark eyes opened to fix on her. "With you."

"Me? What did I do?"

"I am not an idiot. You left a male who chose another female over you. You have no forgiveness for such things. Did you honestly believe I would accept her offer of intercourse?" He growled low in his throat.

"You really need to stop doing that."

"Being logical?"

"Growling. It ruins that whole cyborgs-are-way-better-than-humans motto you always spout. What was I supposed to think when I walked out here to see her pawing you? Did you notice that she didn't have any clothes on? Another minute and she would have climbed you like a tree."

He gaped at her, mute.

"What?"

"A tree?" Zorus still looked baffled.

"You're damn tall. Use your imagination to figure that one out." She tried to calm down. Maybe the situation wasn't as bad as she'd thought but the sight of a naked cyborg attempting to seduce Zorus had temporarily made her go with emotion rather than reason. She'd already been upset anyway. "Never heard that saying, huh?"

"Charlie…" Zorus faced her head on. "You do not trust me if you believed I wanted to have intercourse with that woman. I do not."

"You just admitted, not five minutes ago, that you regret bringing me here."

His dark gaze widened. "I made no such statement."

"Didn't you?" She sighed. "Look at what I've cost you. You said you need to assess things, which tells me that you're sorry you brought me home with you. Let's not bullshit each other after we've been totally honest so far. I've brought you nothing but trouble since we landed on this planet. Your son is pissed, your council embarrassed you, and I'm sure you're wondering what the hell you were thinking by hooking up with me."

The anger melted from his face. "Charlie—"

She held up her hand. "I don't need a roof to fall down around me to see daylight. The view is pretty darn clear." Her hand dropped to her side.

"I do not regret bringing you with me."

"Right. Sure. That's why you're so happy right now that I'm living with you."

"I am happy that you are here."

She wanted to believe him desperately. "You don't look it and I don't blame you."

"I'm trying to come to terms with the things that have changed. My feelings for you haven't. That's what I meant. You took my words wrong. The only certainty in my life at this moment is you." He took a step closer. "Come here." His arms opened.

194

Charlie moved before she could think. She walked right into his body to wrap her arms around his waist. He hugged her close, his chin rested on the top of her head, and she fought back tears.

"I love you." He spoke softly. "I need to be clearer with my thought processes to avoid further misunderstandings. I am debating leaving the council since I am not certain I want them to torment me on a daily basis. The probability of it is high. I worry that my son will cause more difficulties for us and I need to find a way to make him understand your value to me. I won't trust him until that has been established."

"You love your job, don't you?"

He hesitated. "Yes. I enjoy my work."

"Then deal with the shit. It will pass. They will grow bored of teasing you. Don't quit your day job. I doubt I could support us on slave wages."

He suddenly chuckled. "Your sayings always amuse me and I appreciate your attempt at humor."

"Who is kidding?" Her chin lifted until she met his gaze. "I'm property here."

Zorus' humor fled. "I no longer am happy about the status of humans on Garden."

"Then change the laws. It's what your council does, right?"

A glint flickered in his gaze. "Yes."

"So stay at your job and work on making me more than something you own."

"You're very smart."

She couldn't resist smiling. "For a human, you mean?"

He softly growled. "Don't do that. I would punish anyone who dared to insult you that way."

"Sorry. Stop growling and I'll stop making smartass remarks. It was a joke."

"It wasn't humorous. Some of my people wouldn't be happy with that law being changed but it wouldn't affect many. There are currently less than thirty humans living on Garden."

"That's so few. How many cyborgs live here?"

"Thousands." He gently released her but kept hold of her hand to lead her to one of the chairs. He sat and spread his thighs, indicating he wanted her to sit. "We are fine now, aren't we?"

She curled up on his lap. "Yes. I'm just sorry for all the grief you're getting over me."

"I'd rather take it than the alternative of not having you in my life. I'm sorry for the miscommunication. We will have them but we need trust, Charlie."

She hesitated. "You've slept with Alis in the past, haven't you? She said something that implied it."

"Yes." His mouth tensed into a grim line. "It was before I met you. That's how favors are exchanged. I mentioned this to you before."

"Yeah. I remember." Her fingers traced his jawline and then she looked deeply into his eyes. "You were really an asshole once, weren't you?"

His eyebrows shot up.

"That's kind of shitty to bargain with women to have sex with you."

"I never pressed them to offer me intercourse. You witnessed her actions. She came here on her own, removed her clothing, and would have attempted seduction if I didn't have you in my life."

"So you're a victim?" She smirked.

"Charlie, are you upset that I had intercourse with Alis in the past? I must point out that it was before we met and I never foresaw you being a part of my life. I will never allow another female to bargain with me in that manner again. You are the only female who has permission to touch me. I would never risk losing you and you are the only one I want."

She snuggled against his big body. "I'm a bit jealous. She had a really nice body."

"I did not notice."

She snorted. "Right. What happened to honesty?"

"I noticed but I find your pale, creamy skin much more attractive and your softness fascinates me. Your body makes me more aroused than I have ever experienced." He didn't look away from her while he spoke. "No other woman has ever affected me the way you do. I've never wanted any female as much as you, Charlie. That is the truth."

"I believe you." She beamed. "You're super hot yourself and no one compares to you."

His head turned and he groaned.

"What?"

"Someone is coming. If that female has decided to try to seduce me again I will lock her inside the elevator for a few hours to cool her down."

"How do you…oh, that's right. You can link to your system without touch. Doesn't it tell you who is there?"

"We don't have cameras on Garden. We hate them after being on Earth. It reminds us of our captivity. When it reaches our floor they will convey a message signal to me if I don't automatically open the doors."

A minute passed and suddenly Zorus tensed. He stood and eased Charlie to her feet in front of him. "Go to our room now. This is cyborg business and it is not a female."

The stern look on his face told her something serious was about to go down. She hesitated.

"Please, Charlie. This is council business. It's classified and has nothing to do with us."

"Okay."

She headed for the bedroom but she turned at the hallway when the elevator doors opened. A black-haired, tall cyborg wearing all black leather entered the apartment. She'd seen him before on the shuttle they'd transferred to when the cyborgs had paid off the human who had brought them from Earth.

"Onyx," Zorus addressed him. "What has happened?"

Charlie wanted to eavesdrop but then kept right on going to the bedroom. She even closed the door though curiosity pricked her. She walked over to stare out window.

* * * * *

"Are we certain?" Zorus tried to suppress his worry.

Onyx grimly nodded. "No doubt about it. When we heard about the attack on Belta Station we investigated since it's the closest one to us. The humans were slaughtered but it wasn't pirates who did it. We found pieces of one nonhuman body they'd left behind in a section of the station that was destroyed by a bomb. It was definitely a Markus Model. It appears they must have killed the humans."

"This is alarming. Out of all the stations for them to attack, I won't believe it was coincidental that it happened to be that one."

"That's what I figured too but I wanted to come to you first. We need to call the council together."

"There's no way they could locate Garden from any information they obtained from those humans. We are always careful to conceal our identities."

"They located where we do our main trading. If they start searching, they could eventually find this planet. It may take them a while but I'm alarmed they got this close."

"I am as well."

A chill ran down Zorus' spine. The Markus Model androids were Earth Government's failed attempt to create another workforce of humanoid-looking advanced robotic hybrids by regenerating organic materials. They were to take the place of cyborgs. The Markus Models had once fooled Zorus into believing they wanted asylum but instead they'd wanted to capture cyborgs to trade for their counterparts being held prisoner on Earth.

"We need to be on high alert. From now on we only do deep-space trading far from here. If they are somehow able to track our interaction with humans we need to lead them along a false trail. From now on, we reduce all contact with any and all stations. We'll need to assign sentry ships to warn us if they enter this system. I want the *Star* to return to Garden and the *Rally* is to remain in orbit. I also want the *Vontage* to return. Contact both Flint and Steel and give them my orders. If there's a fight, our priority is defending Garden."

"Agreed," Onyx sighed. "We really don't need more enemies."

"I believed we had destroyed those androids. How is this possible? I was informed by Flint that they were blown up on the Earth shuttle *Nugget* after our life pods launched."

Onyx shrugged. "I don't know. My guess is that more of them escaped from Earth." Onyx paused. "I hope you aren't going to be as stubborn about them as you were in the past. Flint is returning on the *Star* as we speak and fully expects difficulties with you. We don't need to run studies on something that dangerous to figure out how Earth has made advancements in technology. We just need to kill them if they come after us again."

"I learned my lesson." Guilt and a little embarrassment spread through Zorus at the memory of believing the androids would make strong allies against Earth Government. Instead they'd attacked cyborgs and that's how Zorus had ended up on a life pod that had delivered him into the hands of humans on Earth. "I am capable of it."

Onyx nodded. "How is it working out with your human? It's the main topic today—about what happened at the council meeting." A grin curved his lips. "I still can't believe you have one."

"Go ahead. Make a disparaging remark if it makes you content to insult me."

"That wasn't my intention. I used to dislike them too but spending time with Ice and Megan has changed my mind. Megan is pretty terrific. If your human is half as good for you as Ice's wife has been for him, then I just wish you well."

The tension eased from Zorus. "I don't want to discuss Charlie but thank you. I'll meet you at the council building in ten minutes. I have contacted them and they are on their way now."

Onyx frowned. "You did?"

"We have a separate link we use to communicate with each other in emergencies. I've related what you've told me. I need to tell Charlie that I have to attend this meeting. Go."

He watched Onyx leave and then took a few deep breaths. He'd brought Charlie to Garden believing she'd be safe but now they were under a new threat. Those Markus Model androids were dangerous and obviously hunting cyborgs. Their new adversary had succeeded, where Earth Government had not, by attacking a station they used regularly for trading. He didn't believe in coincidences. He went in search of Charlie.

She stood inside their bedroom at the window, staring outside, when he entered. Uncertainty was etched her features when she met his gaze. "Is everything okay?"

He hesitated. "We made an enemy recently who is causing some trouble. I'm sure it will be fine but I need to return to the council building. We need to discuss the threat and take precautions to protect our people immediately."

"Is this about me?"

He pulled her into his arms, inhaling her feminine scent, and rubbed his cheek against the crown of her head when she hugged him back. "No, love. Have you ever heard of Markus Models?"

She paled. "Those are those crazy defense-model androids that were on the news on Earth some weeks ago."

"What did it say?" He made a mental note to have someone hack into Earth's news bulletins to research any mention of the androids. "Do you remember?"

"Something about some of them malfunctioned and a number of employees at a large manufacturing company were killed. Some of the models escaped. They had a photo of what one looked like flashing on vid screens. They wanted the public to notify the authorities if we saw any of them. They were listed as extremely dangerous."

"They want to find cyborgs and use us to trade for the freedom of more of their kind from Earth." He shouldn't have shared that with her but he did it anyway. She was his female and he trusted her. "That's what the meeting is about."

"Thank you for telling me. Are they as dangerous as I heard?"

He remembered the disturbing androids with vivid clarity. They had given him the creeps. "Yes."

"Will they find Garden?"

"No." He hoped not anyway. "We are taking measures to prevent that."

Her body softened in his hold as her fear drained away. "Good."

He brushed a kiss on her temple. "I'll return soon."

"Okay." She eased out of his hold to smile at him. It melted him inside when she looked at him that way. "I'll fix us lunch in about an hour. Think you'll be back by then?"

"I should be." He turned to leave but she suddenly grabbed his hand. He glanced at her as he paused.

"I love you."

Warmth spread throughout his chest as he grinned back at her. "I love you too."

Chapter Thirteen

Charlie had just started lunch for Zorus when she heard the elevator doors slide open. She entered the living room to greet him but instead froze in terror. Darius glowered at her from across the room. Her heart instantly started to pound painfully hard.

"My father has been hung up with the emergency meeting."

She highly doubted Zorus had sent his son to relay a message to her. A sense of dread filled her as she remained in place, unable to move as a result of her fear. He tilted his head.

"That's a beautiful expression on your face. I admit, I'm more than a little aroused by it."

She found her voice. "You're not supposed to be here."

"I'm more than aware and it took me some time to hack into my father's security system. The thing about knowing one's father is learning how his mind works."

"What do you want?" She had a sinking feeling that he wasn't there to spread joy.

"How have you learned to control my father? Are you drugging him? Did your human colleagues put implants inside his brain that make him do as you order?" He started to walk toward her. "You are going to tell me exactly what has been done to him."

"Nothing." She backed up. "You need to leave. Zorus warned you to stay away from me."

Rage twisted his features. "I knew it. You made him do that."

"I didn't. He told me that's what he did." She bumped the table, inched around it, and frantically tried to think of a way to escape. "Please don't hurt me."

"I won't rape you."

That didn't comfort her. Her back hit solid wall and she knew how a trapped animal felt as her gaze darted around the kitchen. She had nowhere to go. The counters blocked her escape. She didn't attempt to make a run for it since she doubted she'd make it past his big, bulky body. Zorus could move fast and the much younger Darius had to be even quicker.

"You are going to come with me peacefully or I will take you unconscious." His hand rose to make a fist. He glanced at it and then her face. "You won't enjoy recovering from broken bones."

"Where are you taking me?"

"I have an acquaintance who is very good at perceiving lies when humans speak them. He owes me a favor. You and I are going to visit his home so he can ask you questions."

"Your father is going to be furious if you hurt me. Please don't do this, Darius. I'm not a spy and I'm not doing anything to your dad. We love each other."

He snorted and came to a halt a foot from her. "My father could never love the thing he hates most."

"I never hurt him and never would." She hoped he could see the truth in her eyes since she made sure not to look away from him.

"Are you going to walk on your own or will you make me harm you?"

"If you want what is best for Zorus, you won't take me. He really does love me. Please think before you do something you'll regret. I'm assuming you want to make sure I don't hurt him but you're the one who is going to cause him grief. He's already torn up over the fight you had over me. He loves you too."

The large cyborg lunged at her. His fingers wrapped into her hair at the base of her neck. He tugged on her to propel he forward but it wasn't painful. Charlie stumbled, in a panic. Darius refused to be reasonable. Zorus would come home to find her gone.

As they passed the table, Charlie hit the plate she'd used for lunch. It slid off the table and crashed to the floor. Broken glass skittered loudly on tile. It didn't even slow Darius. He just shot her a dirty look as he forced her to leave with him.

Charlie didn't fight though she wanted to. Zorus would come for her when he realized she'd been taken. The list of suspects would be short since she'd only been threatened by his son. She just needed to keep Darius from hurting her until she could be rescued. He shoved her into the elevator.

"Please, Darius. Don't—"

"Shut up or I'll hit you."

She pressed her lips tightly together and they rode the elevator down six floors then, to her surprise, it stopped and the doors opened.

"Walk."

"Your friend lives in the same building?"

He growled exactly the way his father did when he was irritated. Charlie grew silent again. She knew she just needed to go along with whatever Darius wanted, to prevent him from harming her. The idea of being hit or having another traumatic scene like the one he'd provided in the bedroom when he'd attacked wasn't something she ever wanted to repeat.

The floor wasn't one big apartment but instead opened up into a hallway with doors spaced widely apart on both sides. He walked her four doors down on the left before he halted. He waited and then the door beeped before it slid open. He released her hair when he gave her a rough push forward.

The male who waited inside scared Charlie more than Darius did. She tried to hide her reaction but knew she failed when icy blue eyes narrowed in anger. The guy had to be six foot seven, had jet-black hair that reached nearly to his waist where it hung free in silky waves, and he'd been damaged badly, judging by the scars on one side of his face. It looked as though something had clawed his cheekbone in two places, leaving thick, white lines to mar what would have been a very handsome face otherwise.

"Krell, this is the female I told you about."

"Zorus will be angry. Are you sure this is a good idea, my friend? Of all the cyborgs you want to avoid pissing off, your father comes foremost to my mind."

Shivers ran down Charlie's spine at the raspy, harsh tone of the cyborg's voice. He flickered his gaze from Darius and then back to her, where his attention remained.

"She's attractive. I can see why your father wants to keep her. She's too small for my personal tastes but I don't have the ego Zorus has."

"Just get her to talk." Darius crossed his arms over his chest, his body planted behind her to keep her from running away, and sounded bored. "If you have to inflict pain, so be it. I want answers as quickly as possible."

Krell moved his head to indicate that Charlie should take a seat in the chair nearest to her. She needed to sit anyway, she reasoned, since her knees wanted to collapse under her. She tried not to gawk at the white scar lines on the man's face. His skin was a pale gray, probably the lightest shade she'd seen on the cyborgs so far. She dropped into the seat.

He wore black breeches with a high-collared, black, soft, long-sleeve shirt. When he drew near, he did it with panther grace. A sense of danger nearly radiated off him. Charlie trembled when she stared up into the coldest eyes she'd ever seen in her life. The ice-blue color wasn't just the cause of her reaction, but they possessed a deadness that lurked in their depths, as if he held no compassion at all.

"I'm Krell," he rasped. "I see you noticed my face." He crouched before her, almost touching her knee. His hand lifted to his throat to peel back the material, to expose the skin there.

Charlie's mouth dropped open and then slammed closed at the sight of the jagged, ugly scar slashed along his throat. She was certain someone, at some point, had tried to slit his throat. It suddenly made his harsh, scary voice understandable. He probably had damage to his larynx from where he'd been cut.

"Humans did this." He released the material and his hand lowered to his waist. He jerked up his shirt to reveal a washboard stomach with muscled ridges. She also noticed more scars but those were thinner lines, at least six of them marked his belly. He dropped the shirt. "And put those on me. I could show you more but I believe I have made my point. I'm not a fan of your kind. You do not want to anger me."

"Okay. I have nothing to hide." She knew her voice had to clue him in on how terrified she felt if her expressions weren't. "I won't lie."

He blinked and then his hand rose. She noticed more scars on the back of his hand, on some of his fingers, and then his warm fingertips brushed her throat. She jerked a little but then forced her body to remain still. His touch returned to gently rest against the side of her throat.

"Are you an Earth spy?"

"No."

"Tell me what you are."

She remembered how important Zorus seemed to deem her status on Earth. "I'm a grunt. I was raised in the Parkway section of the States. I drew the attention of some of the upper class and they donated a scholarship for me to get some schooling. I became a programmer. I'm good at it."

"How did you come into contact with Councilman Zorus?"

"My brother was hired to rescue him from the medical facility where I install security upgrades. He talked me in to helping him. He left me with no choice but to rescue Zorus. I'm a fugitive from Earth now. If the government finds me, they'll execute me."

Krell rubbed her throat gently and his gaze seemed to warm slightly. "Do you love Zorus?"

"Yes."

"Are you plotting to harm or kill him?"

"No!" She glared at him. "I'd never do that."

"I find that very hard to believe. We don't even like him. How is it that you have found something to love about him?"

She drew in a shaky breath. "I know he comes off as a total asshole, but deep down, he's really sweet. I hated him right off the bat when we met. He was rude and full of himself but he grew on me."

Full lips curved slightly upward and he glanced at Darius. "She's telling the truth."

"No," Darius ground out harshly, his temper flaring. "She's using him. She's drugged him or they implanted him."

Krell's fingers continued to trace her skin. He locked gazes with Charlie again. "Are you drugging Zorus?"

"No."

"Is there some way you are able to control him to make him do as you order? Tell me how you would do it if you could. Don't lie to me. Tell me what options you have to do this."

"Why ask her that? Just make her tell what she did, not what she could do."

Krell shot Darius an annoyed look. "Silence. The more she talks the more I can read her." He paused. "Also I enjoy the sound of her voice. Shut up or leave. Your choice. Continue, Charlie."

"No, I'm not controlling him in any way. Is that even possible? At first, I thought he had programming and, trust me, I wanted to hack into his systems to change a few things. That growling he does when he's pissed—" She paused. "Forget that part. I'm not doing myself any favors by admitting that, am I? Anyway, he's more than convinced me that he's got his own mind and is nothing similar to an android. I thought that's what he'd be when I got him out of that holding cell. It nearly messed up the escape I had planned since he was so much bigger than any of the droids I'd ever seen before. The clothes I brought him didn't fit and I had to have him hold me instead of the other way around when we had to be lifted up the side of a building by a cable. There wasn't any way in hell I could have kept hold of him and I sure wasn't about to let him drop to his death. I can only hack into computers and Zorus has a mind. I'm just a programmer, a grunt, and I'm not a spy."

"Is that what humans from your younger generation believe us to be? Androids?"

"Yes."

"Are you and Zorus engaging in intercourse?"

A blush warmed her cheeks. "That's really rude to ask, but considering I've been kidnapped and I'm afraid, I'll answer. Yes. I told you I love him and he loves me." She drew in a deep breath. "Zorus is going to be really pissed if you hurt me. He's really protective of me and possessive."

The ghost of a smile returned. "Possessive? Why did you use that word?"

She wanted to pull away from his fingertips, which had lowered to her collarbone and under the edge of her shirt. "I mean he nearly killed his own son for trying to rape me so please stop letting your hands roam. It's one thing to feel my pulse while you talk to me but now you're exploring. I know the difference."

His fingers froze. The dead, hard look returned when his eyes seemed to grow cold again. His mouth pressed together and his nostrils flared. "Darius attempted to rape you?"

"Yes."

Krell rose to his feet quickly, his touch gone, and glared at the other cyborg. "You never mentioned that to me."

"She's human. She has no authority to say no, therefore I can't force intercourse with her."

"Leave. She's not a spy, she truly loves Zorus, and is no threat to him. She isn't controlling him by any means you feared. If she is a weakness to him it is only from the emotions he feels for her."

"I don't believe that."

"Then you are a fool. Leave, Darius."

"Fine. Get up, human. We're leaving."

Krell took a long step forward, placed his body between where Charlie sat and Darius stood. "She remains here with me."

"I'm taking her with me."

The man dressed in black shook his head, shoved his long, black hair back over his shoulder with one hand, and took a defensive stance. "She isn't going anywhere with you. If you try to take her from me, I'll fight you."

Oh shit! What the hell is going on? Krell braced to fight his friend. She had no idea why he would do that or what his intentions were.

Darius snarled before the two men lunged for each other. Charlie leapt out of the chair and backed into a corner to keep out of the way when the two large cyborgs tangled in the middle of the living room.

* * * * *

The meeting had gone on far longer than Zorus had estimated. While he tended to just issue orders, the other council members wanted to vote on everything meticulously. They'd been a little irritated when they realized he'd already ordered Onyx to contact two of their ships to return home to protect the planet. Three members of the council had backed Zorus to help sway the votes in his favor. Those three had the displeasure of personally having contact with the Markus Models.

Councilman Parlis had argued the hardest, alongside Zorus. They were friends, had been grown in the same cloning laboratory on Earth, and even trained together. After the meeting, they'd had a private talk.

"They are afraid." Parlis hesitated. "So am I."

"I am as well. We need to defend our planet rather than spreading out our resources to hunt them down. It's wiser to wait for them and hit them full force when they come after us."

"I'm just glad you're in agreement with killing these things. I approved of your original decision to study them until I met them firsthand." The other cyborg shivered. "Now I just want to end the threat once and for all."

"I agree." Zorus had shaken his friend's hand. "I need to get home."

"How is it working out with the human female?"

Zorus didn't attempt to hide the smile. "She makes me happy."

"You deserve it."

He'd left then. When he got home, silence greeted him instead of Charlie. "I'm home," he called out loudly. "Charlie?"

Broken glass lay scattered across the kitchen floor. Fear that she'd been cut by it sent him rushing toward their bedroom. Within minutes, he knew she wasn't anywhere to be found in the apartment. Alarm grew into panic. He had to calm enough to link to his security system.

She'd had to hack her way into it to be able to activate the elevator. It took him a good minute to find where she'd managed to penetrate his security. He frowned and then cursed. She hadn't hacked it but he knew who had.

"Darius," he snarled. He linked to outgoing communications to contact his son. When he wasn't able to reach him, his eyes opened, and pure rage burned through his veins.

He rushed for the elevator but then hesitated. Darius wouldn't take her to his home. It would be the first place he'd search. His son would know he'd come after Charlie, would expect it. He closed his eyes to log back in to his security system, hoping to find out how long they'd been gone. It would help him deduce how far they could have traveled inside the city.

The logs to the elevator surprised him. Darius hadn't left the building but had instead gotten off six floors below. He hacked into the building occupant information files to see which cyborgs held residences there. One name made him stiffen. He knew where Darius had taken Charlie.

Rage and fear battled for dominance while he suffered the short elevator ride. Krell had to be the best human interrogator on Garden but he had grown unstable over the years. One thing had become clear. He hated humans after what they'd done to him when they'd realized he'd been helping in the rebellion on Earth. They'd tortured him and then left him to die. The idea of him hurting Charlie made him run when the elevator doors parted.

Zorus didn't knock. He lifted a booted foot instead, his anger fiery hot, and planted it near the electronic lock with all his force. The impact sent the door crashing inward. He stormed inside, only to be brought up short by the sight of Krell and Darius in the midst of a brutal physical altercation. He spotted Charlie pressed tightly into the far corner of the room. He inched around the battling males to reach her.

He evaluated her as he pulled her into his arms, careful to keep his body blocking her from the males. She looked pale and frightened but no visible damage marred her. "Are you unharmed?"

"I'm good."

Zorus held her tighter, grateful he'd located her in time, and then turned his head. Krell had beaten Darius severely but nothing life threatening. Darius had lost his strength and when a punch sent him to the floor, he stayed down. Krell snarled out in victory, ran a bloody-knuckled hand through his long hair, and then turned to glower at Zorus.

"I'm glad you arrived, though you will replace the broken door immediately. I was about to contact you to come collect her. I do not mind asking females questions but I will take no part in the torture of one." Krell shot Darius a disgusted look. "I wasn't about to allow him to leave with her, considering he didn't believe it when I told him she's being truthful."

Zorus shifted Charlie to his side to face the scarred cyborg. "What is going on?"

"Darius said he needed my skills to detect if the female had deceived you. She accused Darius of attempting forced intercourse with her. I do not allow that. He doubted my skills and planned to take her out of here. I don't trust him to guard a female when he has no honor. Any male who uses brutality on a weaker female who has no chance of defense is a coward." Krell suddenly moved and kicked Darius in the stomach. "Those types believe it is fun to harm the weaker opponent. Did you enjoy that, Darius?" He hauled back his foot again but then refrained from landing it on the downed cyborg. "I should kick you in the genitals but I'll refrain. I know you are sterile since we share a breeding pack but Jazel will hold issue with it if I put you out of commission, making you unable to have intercourse with her."

Krell backed away before he gave Zorus a cold look. "Protect your female better. You would never allow another male to harm her without facing your full wrath. I know he is your son but do the right thing this time."

Zorus hid his shock that the fight had been prompted by Krell defending Charlie. He also refrained from wincing when Darius moaned. His son had been beaten badly. "I am contacting security now. They'll take him to medical and then to a holding cell."

"Good." Krell growled the word. "You should have brought her to me immediately to dispel any doubts cyborgs had about her loyalty to you. Emotions are a bitch, aren't they?"

"Yes," Zorus sighed, "they are. You're correct but I wanted to protect Charlie. I trust her but didn't want her to doubt that by having to bring her to you for verification. I didn't need any."

"You're an arrogant son of a bitch who believes just because you say or think something that everyone else should as well." Krell glanced at his split knuckles. "I admire that about you." He pinned Zorus with a cool stare. "But then, I'm a bastard too. Follow protocol next time to avoid an asshole taking things into his own hands, if anyone has doubts about her. You're lucky he brought her to me instead of to someone who might have harmed her."

"Thank you."

Krell nodded. "I am going to go wash off the blood and change my clothing. By the time I am done, I want him gone and someone here to replace that door. You know how I enjoy my privacy." He lowered his gaze to Charlie. "If you decide he's too much of an asshole for you to live with, you're welcome to stay here with me." He spun on his booted feet to stride down a hallway and out of sight.

Charlie leaned more heavily against Zorus. He hugged her tighter, relieved he'd found her so quickly. "I'm sorry."

"We should probably try to help Darius. Your son just got the shit kicked out of him and he's bleeding on the carpet. Think that guy would mind if I raided his freezer for some ice?"

His heart melted even more where Charlie was concerned. She worried about his flesh and blood, despite Darius having come after her again. He knew she did it because she loved him. She was willing to be lenient toward Darius for his sake.

"He did this, he will survive, and I don't want you to give him first aid when he doesn't deserve compassion at this moment. Security is on their way up. One of our doctors will patch him up."

Charlie winced when Darius groaned. "He looks as if he's in a lot of pain. Are you sure we shouldn't put ice on him? His left eye is swelling shut and I think that's one of his teeth on the floor by his elbow."

Zorus sighed. "He made his choice when he disregarded my orders to stay away from you. I am happy Krell didn't kill him but he needed to be humbled in this way. I'm actually grateful I am not the one who had to do it. Perhaps this will teach my son a lesson. He had no authority to force you from our home."

Two large cyborgs dressed in black entered the apartment. Zorus eased his hold on Charlie and then swept her up into his arms. She wasn't wearing shoes. The table had been shattered during the fight and he didn't want to risk injury to her feet.

"Arrest him for trespassing into my home and for theft of my…" He grimaced.

"Property," Charlie finished his sentence. "Darius stole me. I belong to Zorus."

Zorus met her gaze. "I will change that law as soon as I'm able."

She nodded, her face rubbing against his shirt. "I know."

Zorus watched the guards gently lift Darius between them. He cuddled Charlie more firmly into his arms to carry her home.

Chapter Fourteen

Charlie nervously ran her hands down the pretty gown. She wished she could ask Zorus if she looked good. He waited in the living room for her to finish getting dressed. The cyborg female, Jove, nodded in approval. Zorus had hired her to make Charlie's clothing.

"The color goes well with your pale skin."

"I feel as if I'm going to throw up," Charlie admitted softly.

"That is normal."

"Right." She swallowed hard and turned to face the other woman. "I never get dressed up this way. I have never owned a dress this beautiful. It's so feminine and I'm just not. I was a tomboy."

"What is that?"

"I grew up dressing and acting as if I were a boy."

"Oh. You look female and very attractive." Jove grinned. "No one would mistake you for a boy now."

"Good." She licked her lips. "I'm ready."

The female nodded. "This gets easier the second and third time you do it."

"Oh no. This is the one and only time for me."

"Didn't Councilman Zorus inform you that you have the ability to take more males into your life? We know he's sterile. You'll need more males to have children."

"I've got Zorus. I have a feeling he's going to keep me occupied enough." She laughed. "He's kind of a big kid sometimes." The memory of him chasing her through the living room the night before flashed. They'd been teasing each other until he had grabbed her and tossed her over his shoulder to carry her off to bed. He loved to play with her.

"I've done this four times."

"Wow. Four, huh?" Charlie paused next to the tall woman. "How do you do it?"

"We spend a week with each male, never live with them at the same time, and it gives me little time with each to cause less friction. Males are good at driving females crazy."

"Do you have a favorite? I mean, one of them has to own your heart the way Zorus does mine."

A sad look crossed the woman's face. "We care, but love?" She shook her head. "It's rare to end up joined by strong emotions and rarely works out well once jealousy arises. The males have to share females, they keep their hearts separated, and so do we. Times are changing though as our numbers increase. One day our children will enter into family units with just one partner. I believe then they'll allow love to grow."

"That's..." Charlie didn't want to say the word "sad" aloud in case she somehow managed to insult the woman.

"I know. We are aware that it's not the way it should be or even how we wish it to be. We adapt. That is why so many have come here today." She smiled. "I envy you." She made a face. "Even if it is Councilman Zorus. He's not well liked."

"He's an asshole but he's all mine and he isn't that way to me."

Charlie chuckled at the stunned expression on the other woman's face. "I'm ready. Let's do this."

Jove led the way out of the bathroom, through the bedroom, and into the large living room. It stunned Charlie at the mass of cyborgs crowded along the walls. Zorus wore black leather with silver decorations and plating on his shoulders and forearms. He had weapons strapped to his hips and thighs. He looked fierce, sexy, and, as his dark gaze met hers, happy. He smiled at her.

Her trembling legs carried her forward until she stopped in front of him. She had to blink back tears. One of his large, warm hands gently grasped one of hers.

"Are you well, love?" He spoke softly so only she'd hear him.

"I'm happy. I cry sometimes when I feel too much of it."

A white-haired cyborg cleared his throat. He wore a red robe that made his pale, light-gray skin and white hair look a little startling. "We begin."

Zorus nodded at him. "We begin."

Charlie had been coached by Jove about what to say. "We begin," she agreed.

Zorus stretched their joined hands toward the robed cyborg. The man wrapped his gloved fingers around both their wrists and held them tightly together.

"I represent the council today in one body," he spoke loudly. "Zorus and Charlie have been granted permission to join in a family unit. If any here protest that decree, step forward to challenge."

Charlie didn't miss the way Zorus reached for the weapon strapped to his thigh. She tensed, glanced around nervously, but no one approached to fight Zorus. She had dreaded this part when she'd been informed that it would take place. On Earth, someone could protest a wedding, but on Garden they could actually fight over a woman, due to their shortage. A long minute passed before Zorus removed his hand from his weapon.

The hold on their wrists eased until the robed cyborg released them. Zorus helped Charlie lower to her knees and then dropped to his own beside her. They faced the cyborg performing the ceremony. He smiled at them.

"With blessings the council now decrees this union solid." He backed away.

Zorus gripped her hand tighter and Charlie turned her head to stare into his brown eyes.

"Be strong."

"I will be."

Worry twisted his handsome features. "Are you sure, Charlie? You don't have to do this."

"Hey, you changed the law so I'm not property anymore. I'm not exactly a citizen just yet but I have rights now. It's my choice to have this joining ceremony with you and I want to do it the way everyone else does."

He took a deep breath. "Just hold onto me."

"Got it."

His head turned when two cyborg males approached. He turned on his knees to face Charlie. He had to release her hand to pull his shirt up over his head. Bare-chested, Zorus impressed her when she studied his broad shoulders, muscled arms, and firm abs. It was a sight she'd never get tired of. He motioned her forward.

She moved until she pressed against his body, inhaled his scent, and didn't tense when he opened her dress down the back to her waist. Her hair had already been pinned up for the ceremony so it didn't get in the way. He shielded her with his big arms while she helped him free her arms until she clutched the material just over her breasts. The tight middle of the dress kept it from sliding down her hips. Zorus pulled her tighter against his chest, smashing her breasts against him. His lips brushed her forehead while he wrapped his hands over her fisted ones.

"It won't hurt for long. We'll do this together."

"Let's not mention pain, okay?"

He chuckled. "Here we go. Don't tense up."

Something heavy draped over her bare shoulders, over her upper arms, and around her back. She knew the same was being done to Zorus. She took slow, steady breaths. It was custom to do this in front of witnesses at the ceremony. They didn't need a host of words as they did on Earth. On Garden it came down to actions.

The heavy drape tightened around her body and warmed. It didn't hurt at first but then she felt a slight burning sensation over her skin. She gripped Zorus tighter and he held her hands. She breathed in his scent and then she could smell something burning. She tried not to wince, knowing it was the fat cells being replaced with magnetic ink, just under her skin and his. The cells were harmlessly burned away as the transfer took place. It wasn't as bad as she'd feared but it wasn't pleasant either. The drape cooled and then foreign hands gently removed it.

"Don't touch them," Zorus reminded her. "They will heal quickly."

Curiosity got the better of her and she pulled away from his chest enough to move her arm to peer at the fresh tattoo on that side while she continued to clutch her dress to keep her breasts covered. She wanted a mirror to see it all but knew she'd have to wait for that.

"They look the same as mine," Zorus whispered. "We match."

She studied his skin and saw the fresh impressions that hadn't been there before. It was a pretty design, written in the cyborg language she couldn't read. Their symbols were artistic, similar to tribal tattoos on Earth, and she smiled at him. He hadn't been branded for his first wife but he'd done it for Charlie.

"So now what?"

He started to help her carefully put the dress back on. The loose material wouldn't irritate the branding. "Now our life as a family unit begins."

Charlie grinned up at him. "Awesome."

He laughed. "Yes, awesome."

"We get a honeymoon, don't we? I forgot to ask about that part. The prospect of you having to get into a fight to marry me kind of shoved it out of my head until now."

225

"I've taken two weeks off from my duties to be with you."

She grinned. "That's so sweet."

Desire flashed in his beautiful eyes. "You don't want me to lie to you. It wasn't something I did to make you happy. I have my own selfish reasons." His focus lowered down her body, taking in every inch he could, while his grin widened. "I plan to remove that gown as soon as our guests leave and I doubt you'll wear anything until I return to my duties."

Zorus rose to his feet and helped her rise. Guests politely clapped to celebrate their joining. Charlie looked around the room with a smile. It had to be the mellowest wedding she'd ever been to besides the whole possible-fistfight clause in the beginning and getting tattoos.

"So what do you do at these things? Where's the booze and the loud music?"

The aghast expression on Zorus' face answered her.

"No booze and dancing?"

"No."

"Then what do you do at these things?"

"We feed our guests, thank them for coming, and then they leave."

"Oh geez." Charlie sighed. "You people are missing out."

"Sorry." He chuckled. "You're not on Earth anymore." His arm wrapped around her waist. "They should be gone within the hour." He winked. "We'll be alone."

She grinned back at him. "Let's feed them and get them out then." She tried to step away to ask the cyborgs who had come to serve food to start passing it out but Zorus spun her inside his arms instead. His mouth came down on hers.

Charlie kissed him back until she couldn't think. To her, all that existed inside the room were his warm lips, his tongue teasing her, and then he pulled away with a glint of humor in his beautiful eyes.

"I love you, Charlie."

"I love you too, Zorus."

"Thank you for bringing me happiness. I'm so glad to have you in my life."

She loved that he hadn't put his shirt back on as her hands rubbed his bare chest. "Thank me when we get them the hell out of here. You can drop to your knees and show me how grateful you are," she teased.

Zorus chuckled. "Just to say the words?"

"Nope. I want tongue."

"I see. And are you thankful and grateful for having me in your life?"

"You are the best thing that's ever happened to me. That's why I plan to drop to my knees after you get up off the floor." She laughed. "To thank you, that is, and I promise to use my mouth but I doubt there will be any words. You're kind of big to talk around."

All humor left his handsome face. "Let's get them the hell out of here."

"Yeah. Let's do that."

They shared a smile before they stopped embracing, then turned to their guests.

48769709R00141

Made in the USA
San Bernardino, CA
05 May 2017